# WILL OF THE SOUL

## Author's Note

Will of the Soul was born long before it became a novel.

I grew up listening to stories shared across towns and families. Stories of lives shaped by unseen forces. Stories people explained using words like karma, justice, and divine intervention. Someone suffered without reason. Someone was protected without effort. Someone paid a price they never knew they owed. And when logic failed, people simply said it was meant to be.

These ideas stayed with me.

They fascinated me not as beliefs, but as narrative forces. I began imagining a world where karma was not abstract, where justice was not delayed, and where the unseen hand people spoke of truly influenced events. A world where choices echoed beyond intention, and consequences arrived not as punishment, but as understanding.

This story was originally conceived as a film screenplay. Images came before words. Silence carried weight. Spaces spoke louder than dialogue. Characters revealed their past through presence rather than explanation. While shaping this work into a novel, I have tried to preserve that cinematic experience, allowing scenes to unfold visually and emotionally, as if the reader is witnessing the story on screen.

Artificial intelligence has been used only as a tool in this process, not as a voice. The imagination, intent, and soul of the story remain human. AI assisted in structuring and refining the narrative, but the questions this novel raises, and the stillness it leaves behind, belong entirely to me.

Will of the Soul does not offer answers. It observes. It watches what happens when people encounter fate, when justice arrives quietly, and when karma reveals itself without warning.

Like the town stories that inspired it, this novel asks only one thing.

What if the soul already knows what is coming.

**-Nanda**

## Characters

### Ajay

He arrives without explanation.
He does not interfere.
He notices what others avoid.
Where he stands, **consequence** becomes visible.

### Jaya Lakshmi

She has ruled through order and restraint.
Silence has been her strongest instrument.
What she protected survived.
What she permitted waited.

### Manasa

She senses before she understands.
Dreams reach her without invitation.
She feels movement beneath stillness.
Her awareness is quiet, persistent, and difficult to deny.

### The Man from the Gardens

He belonged without claiming.
The land recognized him first.
His disappearance marked the beginning of memory.

### The Brother

He lived near the edges of belonging.
Denied slowly.
Lost quietly.
Remembered when absence became undeniable.

### The Estate

It absorbs decisions rather than voices.
It waits longer than people expect.
It does not accuse.
It **remembers**.

## The Painting

A figure beside water.
Neither comfort nor threat.
It does not speak.
It waits until looking becomes unavoidable.

"WHAT WE REFUSE TO FACE DOES NOT DISAPPEAR.
IT WAITS, AND IN WAITING, IT LEARNS HOW TO RETURN."

# CHAPTER ONE

# THE ASSIGNMENT

Ajay learned early that **silence** was not the absence of sound. It was something far heavier. It pressed inward, demanding attention without asking for permission. Noise could be ignored, argued with, or escaped. Silence offered no such choices. It stayed.

The office where he sat that evening had learned this truth well. It was a narrow room on the third floor of a commercial building that existed without identity. Its walls were concrete, painted a color chosen more for tolerance than taste. Heat lingered longer than necessary, as if the structure resisted change. The glass windows reflected more of the inside than the world beyond them, creating the faint impression that the building preferred introspection over participation.

The city continued its restless movement below. Traffic horns rose and fell without rhythm or intention. Vendors called out with rehearsed urgency. Somewhere close by, a radio played an old song whose lyrics had faded into irrelevance while its emotion refused to disappear. None of it demanded Ajay's involvement. The sounds brushed against his awareness and dissolved.

On the table in front of him lay a thin file.

It carried no name. No emblem. No letterhead. There was no attempt at legitimacy, no formal declaration of authority. Only a single word written carefully on the cover.

**Confidential.**

Ajay did not reach for it immediately. Experience had taught him that the impulse to open, to examine, to understand was often premature. Objects revealed more when allowed to exist untouched. Meaning surfaced more clearly when the mind was not rushing to assign it.

Across the table sat the man who had brought the file.

At first glance, he appeared unremarkable. Neither young nor old, neither confident nor uncertain. He was dressed conservatively, not expensively, with the kind of care that suggested intention rather than wealth. His watch was plain. His shoes were polished but worn. Every visible choice seemed designed to avoid attention.

Ajay noticed the details others overlooked. The way the man sat slightly forward, as if prepared to defend himself. The tension in his jaw when he believed he was not being watched. The way his fingers rested together, not clasped, not relaxed, but restrained.

The man cleared his throat.

"You can open it," he said.

Ajay did not respond. His gaze remained on the file, but his attention had shifted inward. He noted the hesitation in the man's voice, subtle but persistent. Hesitation rarely came without reason.

"Before I do," Ajay said calmly, "I need to ask you something."

The man straightened slightly. "Of course."

"Why me"

The question was simple. Its effect was not.

Most people answered that question too quickly. They spoke of qualifications, referrals, professional reputation. Those answers were polished and predictable. This man hesitated.

"I was told," he began, then stopped.

Ajay waited.

"I was told you observe," the man continued. "You do not interfere. You report what you see without becoming involved."

Ajay nodded faintly. That was accurate.

"And you remain calm," the man added. "Even when things become uncomfortable."

Ajay lifted his gaze for the first time.

"**Discomfort** is not **danger**," he said. "People confuse the two because one feels familiar."

The man swallowed.

That was enough.

Ajay placed his hand on the file and opened it.

Inside were several photographs, a few typed documents, and a folded map creased with unnecessary precision. Ajay did not study them immediately. His eyes moved instead to the final page, where a location was printed clearly.

Ooty. Nilgiris.

Something shifted within him. It was not fear. Not curiosity. It felt like pressure, similar to the sensation of changing altitude. Ajay trusted such signals more than logic. Logic explained. **Sensation warned.**

"Who is the client" Ajay asked without looking up.

The man adjusted in his chair. "He prefers not to be named."

"Everyone prefers that," Ajay replied.

"He lives abroad," the man added quickly. "The matter involves family property."

Ajay closed the file.

"No," he said.

The man stiffened. "You have not even reviewed the material."

"I do not take cases involving unnamed clients hiding behind intermediaries to resolve family matters," Ajay said evenly. "Those situations rarely involve **truth**."

The man leaned back slightly. Not in defeat. In relief, as if resistance had been expected.

"It is not a dispute," the man said quietly.

Ajay tilted his head. "Then what is it"

The man leaned forward, lowering his voice even though the room was empty.

**"Deaths."**

Ajay felt the internal pressure return, heavier now.

"How many" he asked.

The man hesitated. "Officially three."

"And unofficially"

The man looked down at the table.

Ajay remained silent. Silence often completed conversations that words could not.

"They occurred years apart," the man said finally. "Different circumstances. No pattern anyone could prove."

"But someone believes there is one," Ajay said.

"Yes."

"And that someone hired a mental hypnotist through an unnamed channel," Ajay added.

"Yes."

Ajay leaned back in his chair.

"Why has nothing been proven legally" he asked.

The man offered a faint, uneasy smile. "Because nothing illegal occurred."

Ajay closed his eyes briefly.

**Nothing illegal.**

Those words carried weight far beyond their simplicity.

“What do you want from me” Ajay asked.

“Observation,” the man replied. “Presence. You will be introduced as a manager overseeing estate operations.”

“Estate,” Ajay repeated.

“Yes. Tea estate.”

The pressure intensified.

“How large”

“Four thousand acres.”

“And the residential land”

“Around a hundred acres. Including a private lake.”

Ajay exhaled slowly.

This was no ordinary assignment.

“Who owns it”

“A woman named Jaya Lakshmi.”

Ajay studied the man carefully now.

“And why is the client not coming himself”

The man hesitated.

“Because he is part of the family,” he said.

“Name.”

"Maha Ganapathi."

Ajay nodded once.

"What exactly am I meant to observe"

"The house. The people. The patterns."

"And the deaths"

"Yes."

"Past or future" Ajay asked softly.

The man did not answer.

Ajay stood and walked to the window. Below, the city continued its movement, unaware of the conversation unfolding above it. People moved with purpose, convinced of direction, unaware of **consequence**.

"I will not prevent anything," Ajay said without turning around.

"That is understood."

"I will not warn anyone."

"Yes."

"And I will leave when I decide observation is complete."

The man nodded.

"One more thing," Ajay said.

"Yes."

"If what I observe implicates your client," Ajay continued, "I will report it exactly as it is."

The man swallowed. "That is acceptable."

They shook hands briefly. The gesture carried no warmth.

After the man left, the room felt quieter.

Ajay remained seated. He did not reread the documents. **Preparation** often interfered with **perception**.

Later that night, he packed carefully. Clothes folded evenly. Nothing unnecessary. At the bottom of the bag lay several paintings wrapped in cloth. They belonged to a former client and had arrived by mistake. Ajay did not unwrap them. He placed them back gently and closed the bag.

Sleep came slowly.

Images surfaced without insistence. A large house partially hidden by mist. A lake too still to feel natural. Endless rows of tea plants disappearing into hills.

Then another image appeared. A long corridor dimly lit. Unfamiliar yet precise.

Ajay observed it without pursuit. It dissolved on its own.

Morning arrived quietly.

As the car carried him away from the city, Ajay felt the air change. Not physically. **Perceptually.** The city loosened its hold. Something else replaced it.

Hours later, the road narrowed. Trees closed in. Mist thickened.

The car slowed.

The bungalow appeared gradually, spread wide across the land rather than rising above it. Verandas extended outward. Windows watched without revealing.

Ajay stepped out.

The air felt heavier here. Deliberate.

The house did not welcome him.

It did not resist him.

It waited.

And Ajay crossed the threshold, unaware that **observation itself** had already begun to alter what he believed he stood outside of.

# CHAPTER TWO

# THE DISCIPLINE OF OBSERVATION

Ajay did not learn **control** by seeking power. He learned it by witnessing collapse.

Years before this assignment, before files without names and conversations that ended in silence, there had been a period when his own mind had refused cooperation. It did not break suddenly. It eroded gradually, like stone worn away by water that never paused. Thoughts multiplied without order. Emotions arrived without cause. Memory lost its sequence and demanded explanation.

He noticed it first during ordinary moments. A pause while speaking. A sentence forgotten midway. A sensation of heaviness without sadness. None of it was dramatic enough to alarm those around him. It was only visible to someone who watched closely.

Ajay watched.

The mind, he realized, did not collapse loudly. It loosened its structure quietly.

Sleep became unreliable. Dreams intruded into waking hours, not as images but as feelings. Familiar places felt distant. Simple decisions demanded disproportionate effort. Yet even then, Ajay did not panic. Panic required surrender. He was not ready for that.

Instead, he observed the deterioration with curiosity.

The problem, he eventually understood, was not emotion itself. It was **identification**.

He had been believing every thought that appeared. He had been accepting every emotion as truth. He had been allowing memory to define meaning without question.

Once that realization formed, it did not bring relief. It brought responsibility.

Responsibility demanded method.

That was how he found the training.

The building stood at the edge of the city, far enough to avoid distraction but close enough to feel reachable. It was modest in appearance, painted a color that resisted description. Neither welcoming nor forbidding. It existed without invitation.

Inside, there were no symbols, no incense, no attempt at mysticism. Just rooms with chairs, open windows, and silence that had been practiced deliberately.

The instructor was an old man whose voice carried no authority. It was not deep or commanding. It did not rise or fall dramatically. It existed in a narrow range, steady and unremarkable.

"You are not here to control minds," the man said on the first day. "You are here to stop being controlled by yours."

Ajay remembered how that sentence had landed. Not as wisdom. As a challenge.

The first days involved no instruction. They involved sitting.

For hours.

Without guidance.

Without correction.

Without reassurance.

Ajay discovered quickly that stillness provoked resistance. Thoughts arrived louder than usual. Memories replayed themselves insistently. Emotions attempted justification. The mind demanded participation.

The instructor did not intervene.

On the third day, Ajay spoke.

"What am I supposed to do"

The old man looked at him briefly. "Notice what happens when you do nothing."

That was the beginning.

Ajay learned that **stillness** was not passive. It was confrontational. It stripped distraction and forced the mind to reveal its habits. The urge to escape became visible. The need for narrative exposed itself.

He watched thoughts arise and fade. At first, he followed them unconsciously. Then, slowly, he learned to pause. To watch without pursuit. To allow sensation without explanation.

Fear appeared as tightness. Sadness appeared as heaviness. Anger appeared as heat.

When not fed with interpretation, they dissolved.

This was not suppression. Suppression required effort and resistance. This was **disengagement**.

Over time, the mind adjusted. Not because it had been defeated, but because it was no longer rewarded with reaction.

Hypnosis, Ajay later understood, was not about entering a trance. It was about recognizing that most people never left one.

People lived inside stories they repeated until belief replaced observation.

Ajay stepped aside.

The training continued for months. There were exercises involving attention, perception, and suggestion, but they were secondary. The core discipline remained the same.

Observe without interference.

Witness without judgment.

Respond only when necessary.

The instructor once said something that stayed with Ajay.

"There are three kinds of people who seek this path," the old man said. "Those who want control. Those who want escape. And those who want clarity."

Ajay did not ask which one he was. He already knew the answer.

Clarity was not comforting. It stripped meaning from suffering without removing sensation. It removed justification without offering alternatives.

It left responsibility intact.

That was why most people avoided it.

Years later, in the present, Ajay stood in the guest room of the estate bungalow, unpacking with the same precision he applied everywhere else. The room was large, its ceiling higher than necessary. Light entered through tall windows that overlooked the tea gardens. The air carried a faint scent of earth and moisture.

He placed his belongings carefully. Clothes folded. Shoes aligned. Nothing left open.

At the bottom of his bag lay the paintings.

He paused.

They had followed him here by accident, yet accidents rarely felt neutral. He did not unwrap them. He acknowledged their presence and moved on.

That was another lesson from training.

Not everything required engagement.

Ajay stepped onto the veranda. The estate stretched outward in disciplined repetition. Rows of tea plants extended toward hills that disappeared into mist. Workers moved quietly in the distance, their motions synchronized by habit rather than instruction.

The **scale** of the land was undeniable. It did not impress him. It pressed upon awareness.

Large spaces did that. They reduced the importance of individual intention.

Ajay breathed slowly.

The bungalow behind him remained silent. He sensed its presence without turning around. Old houses did not speak loudly. They accumulated memory through use and neglect, through decisions made and avoided.

He returned inside.

The corridor leading deeper into the house was long and dim. Light filtered unevenly through windows placed with intention rather than symmetry. His footsteps echoed briefly, then disappeared.

Ajay felt the internal pressure again.

Not discomfort.

Recognition.

That sensation had accompanied him before significant shifts in life. It did not predict outcome. It signaled **threshold**.

He paused near the end of the corridor.

The central hall lay beyond, though he had not yet been invited inside. The air felt different there, heavier, charged with something unresolved.

Ajay did not proceed.

He had learned not to rush thresholds.

Instead, he turned and returned to his room.

As evening approached, sounds from the estate grew clearer. Machinery from distant tea factories hummed steadily. Wind moved through the gardens with measured consistency. Somewhere, water shifted gently.

Ajay sat on the edge of the bed and allowed his attention to settle.

Training had taught him that environments spoke continuously. Most people were too busy interpreting to listen.

He listened.

That night, sleep came unevenly. Not restless, but light. Images surfaced without insistence. The lake appeared again, still and reflective. A corridor stretched longer than memory allowed. Faces remained indistinct.

Ajay observed each image without pursuit.

They dissolved.

Morning arrived with mist clinging to the land. Ajay woke early and stepped outside. The air was cool, heavy with moisture. Workers moved quietly, their routines uninterrupted by his presence.

No one asked questions.

That was intentional.

Observation required invisibility.

As he walked along the edge of the gardens, Ajay felt something settle within him. Not comfort. Alignment.

This place demanded patience. It did not reward haste.

He understood then why he had been chosen.

Not because he could control minds.

Because he could **remain**.

Remain when others fled.

Remain when clarity arrived without mercy.

Remain when truth did not ask permission.

Ajay returned to the bungalow as the mist began to lift.

The house waited.

And he, trained to witness without interference, understood that his role here was not to change what would unfold.

It was to see it clearly.

# CHAPTER THREE

# THE AGREEMENT OF SILENCE

The first meeting with Jaya Lakshmi did not happen immediately.

Ajay noticed this before he was told.

The delay was deliberate, not logistical. Staff moved around him with efficiency but without urgency. Meals arrived on time. Instructions were conveyed politely through intermediaries. No one mentioned her name unless necessary. When they did, their voices lowered slightly, as if volume itself required permission.

Power announced itself most clearly through absence.

Ajay understood that.

He had seen it before in corporate offices, government buildings, family homes where authority rested not on presence but on expectation. The longer one waited, the more the waiting itself became a statement.

That afternoon, Ajay was asked to inspect the commercial records of the estate.

The request came through a senior supervisor whose manner was respectful but distant. A man trained to follow instructions without curiosity. Ajay followed him through a side corridor that led away from the residential wing and toward a separate structure that housed the estate offices.

The building stood apart from the bungalow, its design utilitarian and precise. Where the house spread and observed, this place functioned. Windows were smaller. Corridors shorter. Movement purposeful.

Inside, the smell of paper and ink lingered. Ledgers lined shelves with practiced order. Desks were arranged to maximize efficiency rather than comfort. Everything here suggested **control**.

Ajay sat across from the supervisor as files were placed before him.

"These are the operational records," the man said. "Production, exports, labor allocation."

Ajay nodded and began to examine them.

Numbers revealed patterns without emotion. Profits rose steadily. Exports increased year after year. The estate was prosperous, well managed, outwardly impeccable.

Yet something felt incomplete.

The records were clean. Too clean.

No disputes. No anomalies. No disruptions significant enough to leave a trace.

Ajay made no comment.

Observation did not require immediate response.

After an hour, the supervisor cleared his throat.

"Madam will see you now," he said.

Ajay closed the file and stood.

They walked back toward the bungalow through a covered passage that connected commerce to residence without forcing interaction. Ajay noted the architecture. Separation of function was rarely accidental.

The central hall awaited him.

It was larger than he had expected. Not grand in ornamentation, but expansive in proportion. The ceiling rose high, supported by beams that bore the marks of age without weakness. Portraits lined the walls, their frames darkened by time. Faces looked outward, expressions frozen in varying degrees of restraint.

Jaya Lakshmi stood near the far end of the hall.

She did not turn immediately.

Ajay waited.

She was tall, her posture erect without rigidity. Her hair was tied neatly, streaked with gray that had not been concealed. She wore a simple sari, its fabric chosen for quality rather than display. Jewelry was minimal, deliberate.

When she turned, her gaze met Ajay's without hesitation.

"You are the manager," she said.

"Yes," Ajay replied.

Her eyes held his for a moment longer than necessary.

"You have come from far," she said.

"Yes."

She gestured toward a chair.

"Sit."

Ajay did.

She remained standing.

"I was told you would oversee operations," she said. "Ensure everything runs smoothly."

"That is my role," Ajay said.

Her gaze flickered briefly toward the portraits.

"This estate has been running smoothly for decades," she said. "We do not tolerate disruption."

Ajay nodded.

"Then my presence will not disturb it," he said.

Her expression tightened slightly.

"We shall see."

She moved to the opposite chair and sat. For the first time, Ajay noticed the faint tension in her hands. Not nervousness. Control maintained through effort.

"You have reviewed our records," she said.

"Yes."

"And you found them satisfactory."

"Yes."

She watched him carefully.

"You ask few questions," she said.

"I observe first," Ajay replied.

"Observation can become interference," she said.

"Only when followed by action," Ajay said.

Her lips curved into something close to a smile.

"You speak carefully."

"I listen carefully."

Silence followed.

It was not uncomfortable. It was deliberate.

"You will stay in the guest wing," she said. "You will report to me directly."

"Yes."

"You will not speak to workers unnecessarily," she continued. "Instructions are passed through supervisors."

"Yes."

"You will not explore areas unrelated to your role," she said.

Ajay looked at her calmly.

"I walk where my responsibilities require," he said.

Her gaze sharpened.

"Responsibilities can be interpreted broadly."

"So can restrictions," Ajay replied.

Another pause.

She leaned back slightly.

"You are here because someone asked for you," she said. "Someone who believes your presence will bring clarity."

"Yes."

"You should understand something," she said. "This house does not reveal itself easily."

Ajay met her gaze.

"Nothing worth understanding does," he said.

She studied him for a long moment.

Then she nodded.

"You may begin tomorrow," she said.

The meeting ended without ceremony.

As Ajay left the hall, he felt the portraits watching him. Not with accusation. With recognition.

That evening, Manasa observed Ajay for the first time.

She stood near the veranda overlooking the lake, her posture relaxed but her attention focused. Ajay sensed her presence before he saw her.

She was younger than he had expected. Her face held softness, but her eyes carried weight. Grief had shaped her features without diminishing them.

"You are new," she said.

"Yes."

"You do not look lost," she said.

"I rarely am."

She nodded, as if that answered something she had not spoken.

"The lake is calm today," she said.

Ajay followed her gaze.

"Yes."

"It is not always," she added.

He did not respond.

She looked at him again.

"You are quiet," she said.

"I listen."

She hesitated, then smiled faintly.

"That is rare here."

She turned and walked away.

Ajay remained by the veranda for a moment longer.

The lake reflected the sky with unsettling precision.

Stillness, he had learned, often preceded movement.

That night, the estate settled into its routines.

Lights dimmed gradually. Machinery slowed. Voices softened.

Ajay lay awake, listening.

Not to sound.

To absence.

Something had shifted.

Not visibly. Not dramatically.

But the **agreement of silence** had been established.

And silence, once accepted, did not release its hold easily.

# CHAPTER FOUR

# THE HOUSE THAT WATCHES

Ajay woke before dawn, not because of sound, but because the **house** had shifted.

It was not a movement he could define. No door had opened. No footstep echoed. Yet something within the walls had adjusted, as if awareness itself had changed position. Ajay remained still, eyes open, allowing the sensation to settle before thought attempted explanation.

The ceiling above him was high and pale, marked faintly by age. Hairline cracks traced paths that spoke of time rather than damage. The room was quiet, but not empty. Silence filled it with intention.

Ajay rose and dressed without hurry. The air carried a coolness that clung to the skin longer than expected. He opened the window slightly. Mist hovered low over the gardens, blurring distance and reducing certainty. Shapes softened. Edges disappeared.

The estate revealed itself most clearly at this hour.

He stepped into the corridor.

It extended farther than memory allowed, its length interrupted by doorways that led to rooms still asleep. The floor beneath his feet was smooth, worn by decades of movement. Each step produced a muted echo that seemed to dissolve before reaching the end.

Ajay walked slowly, attentive to how the space responded.

Architecture, he had learned, was never neutral. It guided behavior, directed attention, imposed rhythm. This corridor was not designed for haste. Its length demanded patience. Its turns discouraged certainty.

He paused near a window that overlooked the inner courtyard. The courtyard was empty, its stone surface damp with morning moisture. Plants lined the edges, their leaves darkened by dew. The air there felt heavier, enclosed by walls that rose just high enough to limit escape.

Ajay understood then that the house had been built not to impress, but to **contain**.

Contain sound. Contain movement. Contain consequence.

He continued walking.

As he moved deeper into the house, the temperature shifted subtly. Cooler near the outer walls. Warmer toward the center. The central hall lay ahead, though he did not enter it yet. He sensed its presence as one sensed pressure before weather changed.

Instead, he turned down a side passage that led toward the rear wing.

Here, the rooms were smaller. Functional. Likely once occupied by family members whose names had faded from relevance. Some doors were closed. Others stood slightly ajar, revealing interiors stripped of personal detail.

Ajay noted the absence.

Rooms were not abandoned accidentally. They were emptied intentionally.

He stopped before one such doorway.

Inside, the furniture was minimal. A bed. A chair. A cupboard that had not been opened in years. Dust lay undisturbed on surfaces, yet the air did not feel stale.

Memory, he realized, did not require objects to persist.

It required space.

Ajay stepped back into the corridor and continued on.

By the time he reached the far end, morning had begun to assert itself. Light filtered in more confidently. Shadows retreated.

The house adjusted.

He returned to the central hall.

Now fully visible, it commanded attention without demanding it. The hall was wide, its proportions balanced deliberately. The floor was polished but not reflective enough to distort. Light entered through tall windows, diffused and restrained.

Portraits lined the walls.

Ajay approached them slowly.

Faces stared outward, expressions fixed in states that resisted interpretation. Some carried authority. Others restraint. A few bore something closer to regret. Their eyes followed no one. They existed to be remembered, not to engage.

He stopped before one portrait in particular.

The man depicted there was older, his gaze direct but tired. His posture suggested responsibility rather than dominance. Ajay felt a faint pressure in his chest.

Not recognition.

Alignment.

He moved on.

Behind him, footsteps echoed softly.

Jaya Lakshmi entered the hall without announcement.

"You are awake early," she said.

"Yes."

She stood near the entrance, observing him as he had observed the portraits.

"The house does that," she said. "It wakes people before they intend to rise."

"Habit," Ajay replied.

She smiled faintly.

"Or memory."

She gestured toward the portraits.

"These are the ones who built what you see," she said. "They believed permanence came from land."

"And did it" Ajay asked.

She considered the question.

"It came from control," she said.

Ajay did not respond.

She walked toward the center of the hall.

"You will begin your duties today," she said. "Supervisors will report to you. You will see the factories later."

"Yes."

She paused.

"You walk the house freely," she said. "Few do."

"I listen," Ajay replied.

Her gaze sharpened briefly.

"Listening reveals more than sight," she said.

"Yes."

Another silence settled between them.

"You should know," she continued, "this house has witnessed much. It remembers even when people forget."

"Memory persists without permission," Ajay said.

She looked away.

“Be careful what you allow it to remember,” she said.

She left without another word.

Ajay remained standing in the hall long after she had gone.

The portraits watched.

Not with judgment.

With **patience**.

Later that day, Ajay accompanied a supervisor through the factory complex. The building was large, its interior humming steadily. Machines moved with measured consistency. The air carried the scent of processed leaves and moisture.

Production flowed without interruption.

Yet Ajay noticed the rhythm.

It mirrored the estate itself. Controlled. Repetitive. Predictable.

He sensed no urgency here. Only momentum.

As they walked, a worker glanced briefly in Ajay’s direction, then away. The look carried no curiosity. Only awareness.

The estate knew he was present.

That evening, Ajay returned to the bungalow as mist began to gather again. The house absorbed sound differently now. Echoes lingered longer. Distances felt extended.

He walked once more through the corridor.

This time, he noticed something he had not before.

A faint change in temperature near one door.

He stopped.

The door was closed. No sign marked it as distinct.

Ajay placed his hand on the wood.

It was cool.

He withdrew his hand without opening it.

Some thresholds did not require crossing to be understood.

He returned to his room and sat quietly as night settled.

From somewhere deep within the house, a sound reached him.

Not a noise.

A shift.

As if a long held breath had been released.

Ajay closed his eyes.

The house was no longer merely a structure.

It was an **observer**.

And Ajay, trained to witness without interference, understood that the first disturbance had already occurred.

It had not arrived with spectacle.

It had arrived with awareness.

# CHAPTER FIVE

# THE GARDENS THAT REMEMBER

Morning arrived without declaration. It did not announce itself with light or sound. It emerged gradually, as if the estate had decided to allow visibility only after certainty had settled.

Ajay stepped out just as the mist began to thin. The tea gardens unfolded before him in disciplined repetition, rows extending farther than the eye could hold comfortably. Each plant stood trimmed to uniform height, shaped by decades of routine. The land did not invite admiration. It demanded attention.

He walked slowly, allowing the rhythm of the place to assert itself.

The gardens were alive, but not expressive. Movement occurred quietly. Workers bent and straightened with practiced efficiency, baskets filling leaf by leaf. Their motions followed patterns learned early and repeated without question. No voice rose above necessity. No gesture exceeded function.

Ajay noticed how the land shaped behavior.

Large spaces reduced urgency. Endless repetition discouraged expectation. The gardens did not reward haste. They absorbed it.

He followed a narrow path that cut between rows. The soil beneath his feet was dark and moist, yielding slightly with each step. It held the imprint of movement briefly, then erased it.

Impermanence was built into the land.

A supervisor walked a short distance behind him, careful not to intrude. The man spoke only when spoken to, his presence designed to facilitate rather than influence.

"These fields are divided by section," the supervisor said when Ajay finally turned. "Each team is assigned a fixed area."

Ajay nodded.

"How long have they worked here" he asked.

The supervisor hesitated.

"Some for decades," he said. "Others since childhood."

"And they stay" Ajay asked.

"Yes."

"Why"

The supervisor considered the question.

"This land feeds them," he said. "It also binds them."

Ajay looked back at the rows.

Binding did not always require chains.

They walked deeper into the gardens. The slope increased slightly. From this elevation, the estate revealed its true scale. The repetition extended outward until it blurred into hills and mist. The gardens appeared endless, yet every plant was accounted for.

Order imposed upon nature always carried cost.

Ajay stopped near a point where the land dipped gently before rising again.

"What happened here" he asked.

The supervisor looked confused.

"Here"

"Yes."

The man hesitated, then shook his head. "Nothing, sir."

Ajay did not press.

The land carried memory regardless of acknowledgment.

They continued walking.

As the sun rose higher, the mist lifted reluctantly. Light sharpened edges. Distance returned. With clarity came heat. Workers adjusted their pace instinctively, shifting weight, altering rhythm without instruction.

Ajay observed how the estate functioned as a single organism. Gardens fed factories. Factories fed commerce. Commerce fed authority. Authority fed control.

Everything returned to land.

At midday, Ajay walked alone.

He followed a path that led toward the lake. The air changed as he approached. Cooler. Heavier. Sound softened as if absorbed.

The lake revealed itself slowly, framed by trees that leaned inward. Its surface was still, reflecting the sky with unsettling accuracy. No ripples disturbed it. No birds skimmed its surface.

Ajay stopped at the edge.

Water held memory differently than land. It did not erase. It layered.

He watched his reflection briefly, then looked away.

Behind him, a voice spoke softly.

"You should not stand there too long."

Ajay turned.

Manasa stood a few steps away, her posture relaxed but attentive. She did not approach closer.

"Why" Ajay asked.

"The lake remembers," she said.

"So do gardens," Ajay replied.

She smiled faintly.

"Yes," she said. "But the gardens forget faster."

They stood in silence.

"You walk the estate as if you are listening," she said.

"I am."

She nodded.

"Then you will hear it soon," she said.

"Hear what"

She hesitated.

"The shift," she said.

Ajay watched her carefully.

"Does it frighten you" he asked.

She considered the question.

"It exhausts me," she said.

They parted without further words.

That evening, the first irregularity occurred.

It was minor. Easily dismissed.

A worker collapsed in the gardens.

Not dramatically. No cry. No sudden fall. He simply sat down and did not rise again.

By the time help arrived, he was conscious but disoriented. He spoke of dizziness. Of heat. Of pressure behind his eyes.

The supervisors attributed it to exhaustion.

Ajay watched from a distance.

He noted the location.

The same dip in the land.

The worker recovered by nightfall. No report was filed. No disruption acknowledged.

Yet the gardens had reacted.

The rhythm had faltered briefly.

Ajay returned to the bungalow as dusk approached. The house absorbed him without resistance. Inside, lights were already lit. Corridors glowed softly, guiding movement without revealing destination.

Jaya Lakshmi stood near the veranda overlooking the gardens.

"You walked far today," she said.

"Yes."

"The gardens demand endurance," she said.

"They demand memory," Ajay replied.

She turned toward him.

"Memory fades," she said. "Land renews."

"Only when allowed," Ajay said.

Her gaze hardened briefly.

"You speak as if the land decides," she said.

"Land always decides," Ajay replied. "People negotiate with consequences."

She studied him in silence.

"Be careful," she said finally. "The gardens are not sentimental."

"No," Ajay agreed. "They are **precise**."

That night, Ajay dreamed.

Not images. Sensations.

Pressure beneath his feet. Weight pressing upward. Breath held too long.

He woke before dawn, heart steady.

The gardens lay silent beyond the window.

Waiting.

The first outward ripple had occurred.

It had not demanded attention.

But it had been **noticed**.

# CHAPTER SIX

# THE WRONG LUGGAGE

Ajay noticed the bag only after everything else had been placed where it belonged.

It stood near the corner of the room, slightly apart from his other luggage, its surface marked by a faint crease that did not match the wear of the rest. He had passed it twice without acknowledgment, registering its presence without examining it. Only when the room settled into order did the bag draw attention.

Disruption revealed itself most clearly in stillness.

Ajay approached it slowly.

The bag was not unfamiliar. Its color, its size, even the weight he remembered carrying were consistent with memory. Yet something about it resisted integration. It did not align with intention.

He knelt and unzipped it partway.

Inside were the paintings.

Wrapped carefully in thick cloth, layered to prevent damage. The smell of aged canvas and varnish lingered faintly, distinct from the scent of clothes and paper. Ajay closed the zipper without unwrapping them.

He did not feel surprise.

Mistakes rarely announced themselves with urgency. They waited to be noticed.

Ajay sat on the bed and allowed the awareness to settle. The paintings had traveled with him by accident. That much was true. He had not planned to bring them. Yet their presence here felt neither intrusive nor neutral.

It felt **timed**.

He had learned long ago not to argue with timing.

The paintings belonged to a former client, a collector whose interest in history had bordered on obsession. Ajay remembered the man clearly. Soft spoken. Excessively precise. A man who spoke of ownership as if it were responsibility rather than privilege.

The paintings had been entrusted to Ajay temporarily while certain arrangements were made. Ajay had accepted without curiosity. Art had never demanded his attention. He respected craft but remained unmoved by symbolism.

Now, standing in this house, the bag felt heavier than it should have.

Ajay left it where it was.

The house had already taken note.

Later that afternoon, a domestic staff member knocked softly and informed him that Jaya Lakshmi would meet him in the evening. Ajay acknowledged the message and continued reviewing reports. The factories operated without interruption. The gardens followed routine. Nothing outward had shifted.

Yet the bag remained present in his awareness.

As evening approached, Ajay changed and stepped into the corridor. The house felt different at this hour. Shadows lengthened. Sound traveled farther. The walls seemed to absorb warmth and release memory.

The central hall was lit sparsely. Lamps along the edges cast a muted glow, leaving the ceiling in partial darkness. Jaya Lakshmi stood near one of the tall windows, her back to the room.

"You wanted to see me," Ajay said.

She turned.

"Yes," she replied. "I was told you brought something unusual with you."

Ajay did not react immediately.

"What were you told" he asked.

"Staff talk," she said. "They notice details."

Ajay nodded.

“I have some paintings,” he said. “They were brought by mistake.”

Her eyes sharpened.

“Paintings,” she repeated.

“Yes.”

“Where are they”

“In my room.”

She considered this briefly.

“You collect art” she asked.

“No.”

“Then why keep them”

“They are not mine to discard,” Ajay said. “They belong to someone else.”

Her gaze lingered on him longer than necessary.

“You should show them to me,” she said.

“Why”

“I appreciate old things,” she replied. “They carry weight.”

Ajay paused.

“I can show them tomorrow,” he said. “If you wish.”

She smiled faintly.

“Yes,” she said. “Tomorrow.”

The decision settled between them.

That night, Ajay slept lightly. The bag remained unopened. Images surfaced briefly, indistinct but persistent. Colors without form. Figures without faces.

He woke before dawn with a faint pressure behind his eyes. It passed quickly.

Morning arrived under low clouds. The house felt closed in, its corridors darker than usual. Ajay prepared the paintings carefully, unwrapping them one by one.

The first revealed a scene from Greek mythology. A figure stood at the edge of consequence, posture rigid, expression resigned. The colors had darkened with age, but the emotion remained intact.

Ajay studied it briefly.

The second depicted a moment of judgment. A crowd gathered, faces turned away from the act they demanded. Responsibility diffused through number.

The third was quieter. A solitary figure beside water, reflection distorted.

Ajay felt the pressure again.

He wrapped them carefully and waited.

When Jaya Lakshmi entered his room later that morning, she did so without hesitation. Her gaze moved immediately to the paintings.

"You did not mention their origin," she said.

"I was not asked," Ajay replied.

She approached the first painting slowly.

"These are old," she said. "Not decorative."

"No."

She studied the second longer.

"This one," she said, "makes people uncomfortable."

"Yes."

She turned toward him.

"Why"

"Because it shows **choice** without excuse," Ajay said.

Her lips tightened.

She moved to the third painting and stopped.

"This one," she said softly, "should not be kept in a private room."

Ajay watched her.

"Why"

"Because it watches back," she said.

She straightened.

"I want this one placed in the central hall," she said.

Ajay considered the request.

"The hall is public," he said. "These paintings are not."

"They belong where truth gathers," she replied.

Ajay felt the decision settle.

"If that is your wish," he said.

She nodded.

The painting was moved that afternoon.

Staff carried it carefully, unaware of its content, respectful of instruction rather than meaning. When it was placed against the far wall of the central hall, the space adjusted subtly.

Sound changed.

Distance shifted.

Ajay noticed the portraits along the walls first.

They seemed less distant now.

Jaya Lakshmi stood beside him.

"It fits," she said.

"Yes," Ajay replied. "It **belongs**."

She turned toward him.

"You speak as if you did not choose this," she said.

"I did not," Ajay replied. "Nor did you."

Her expression flickered.

That evening, Manasa stood near the hall entrance, staring at the painting from a distance.

She did not approach.

She did not speak.

Her breath had quickened.

Ajay noticed.

"You see it," he said quietly.

She nodded.

"It should not be here," she said.

"Why"

"Because it has already begun," she replied.

"What has"

She shook her head.

"I do not know yet," she said. "But the lake will tell me."

She turned and left.

That night, the house did not sleep.

No doors opened. No voices rose. Yet something moved through the corridors with certainty.

Ajay lay awake, aware.

The painting remained still.

The house watched.

And what had arrived as **wrong luggage** had taken its place with unsettling ease.

## CHAPTER SEVEN

## THE WOMAN WHO OWNS THE HOUSE

Jaya Lakshmi had learned long ago that authority did not require explanation. It required consistency. She practiced it daily, not as performance but as habit. Habit shaped expectation, and expectation shaped obedience.

Ajay noticed this before she spoke.

It was present in the way staff adjusted their posture when she entered a room. In the slight delay before anyone responded to her presence, as if the house itself paused to confirm alignment. Even silence behaved differently around her. It did not settle. It waited.

She stood in the central hall that morning, facing the newly placed painting. Light from the tall windows reached the canvas unevenly, catching certain details while leaving others in shadow. She did not approach it closely. Distance was part of her method.

"You walk freely," she said without turning.

"Yes," Ajay replied.

"Few do," she said. "Freedom inside this house is misunderstood."

Ajay remained silent.

She turned toward him slowly.

"I have lived here all my life," she said. "I know which spaces welcome movement and which demand restraint."

"Yes."

"You seem comfortable everywhere," she said.

"Comfort is not permission," Ajay replied.

Her eyes narrowed slightly.

"Then what allows you to walk as you do"

"I listen," Ajay said.

She studied him carefully.

"Listening is selective," she said. "One hears what one wishes to hear."

"Or what remains when desire quiets," Ajay replied.

She looked away.

They stood in silence for a moment longer.

"This painting," she said finally, gesturing toward the wall, "has altered the hall."

"Yes," Ajay said.

"You noticed."

"Yes."

She nodded faintly.

"I did not expect that," she said. "Old things often resist relocation."

"This one was waiting," Ajay said.

She did not respond immediately.

"Do you know what it depicts" she asked.

"A moment of reckoning," Ajay replied.

Her lips tightened.

"That word is used lightly," she said. "Reckoning implies justice."

"Yes."

"And justice implies guilt," she added.

"Yes."

She turned to face him again.

"You speak with certainty."

"I observe," Ajay said. "Certainty belongs to those who resist it."

She laughed softly, though there was no humor in the sound.

"You are careful," she said. "Careful men survive here."

"That is not why I am careful," Ajay replied.

She walked toward one of the tall windows and looked out at the gardens.

"This land," she said, "has been ours for generations. It does not forgive weakness."

"Land does not forgive or punish," Ajay said. "It remembers."

Her posture stiffened slightly.

"You repeat that often," she said.

"Because people forget," Ajay replied.

She turned from the window.

"My family built this estate from nothing," she said. "They endured loss, betrayal, hunger. They claimed what others failed to protect."

"Claiming is not the same as deserving," Ajay said.

Silence followed.

It was not empty.

She approached him slowly, stopping just short of intrusion.

"You were not sent here to judge," she said.

"No," Ajay agreed. "I was sent to **observe**."

"Observation becomes judgment when it is remembered," she said.

"Only when guilt is present," Ajay replied.

Her gaze hardened.

"You speak of guilt as if it were visible," she said.

"It is," Ajay replied. "When one stops hiding from it."

She stepped back.

"You should understand something," she said. "This house rewards loyalty."

"Yes."

"And it destroys betrayal," she continued.

"Yes."

"You are here because someone wants answers," she said. "But answers come with cost."

"Yes."

She studied him for a long moment.

"You do not ask questions," she said.

"I wait for them to ask me," Ajay replied.

She nodded once.

"Then wait," she said.

She left the hall.

Ajay remained standing, aware of the painting behind him. The portraits watched without comment. The hall felt heavier than before, its air dense with withheld meaning.

Later that day, Ajay accompanied Jaya Lakshmi through the estate offices. She walked ahead of him, her pace unhurried but deliberate. Staff moved aside instinctively, clearing paths without instruction.

"You will attend the export review this evening," she said. "The figures matter."

"Yes."

"They always have," she added. "Numbers are honest."

"Only when context is acknowledged," Ajay said.

She paused briefly, then continued walking.

In the office, she reviewed documents with precision. Each decision was made quickly, without visible doubt. Ajay watched how authority functioned through repetition. No hesitation. No apology.

Yet beneath the efficiency, he sensed effort.

Control required maintenance.

As evening approached, they returned to the bungalow. The house absorbed their footsteps quietly. Light shifted as clouds moved overhead, altering the hall's atmosphere.

Jaya Lakshmi stopped before the painting once more.

"I did not intend to keep it," she said.

"Yes."

"Yet I insisted," she said.

"Yes."

"Why do you think that is" she asked.

Ajay considered the question.

"Because it reflects without accusation," he said. "It allows recognition without confrontation."

She turned toward him.

"You believe I need recognition" she asked.

"I believe recognition arrives whether invited or not," Ajay replied.

She stared at the painting again.

"You are not afraid of it," she said.

"No."

"Why"

"Because I am not inside it," Ajay replied.

She inhaled slowly.

"People mistake fear for conscience," she said. "They believe discomfort means wrongdoing."

"Discomfort means resistance," Ajay replied. "Resistance often protects something unresolved."

Her hand tightened slightly at her side.

That night, Manasa dreamed for the first time since the painting arrived.

She woke abruptly, breath shallow, heart racing. The image lingered even with her eyes open. Water rippling outward from a single point. Faces forming and dissolving. A sense of **inevitability** she could not escape.

She did not cry out.

She sat up and waited.

Across the house, Ajay woke at the same moment.

He did not know why. There was no sound. No movement. Only a shift in pressure, as if the estate itself had exhaled.

He sat still, listening.

Something had begun to move.

Not in the gardens.

Not in the factories.

Within people.

By morning, Jaya Lakshmi stood again before the painting.

She did not look away.

"You will remain here," she said to Ajay without turning. "Until I decide otherwise."

"Yes," Ajay replied.

"And you will tell me," she said, "if you see anything unusual."

"Yes."

She paused.

"Some things," she added, "are better left unseen."

Ajay met her gaze.

"Only when they have already been accepted," he said.

She looked at him for a long time.

Then she turned back to the painting.

The house remained silent.But silence had shifted from **absence** to **anticipation**.

# CHAPTER EIGHT

## THE DREAM THAT ARRIVES FIRST

Manasa had learned to recognize the moment before sleep failed her.

It arrived not as fear, but as **anticipation**. A tightening behind the eyes. A faint heaviness in the chest. A sense that something had already begun elsewhere and was now making its way toward her. When this sensation appeared, she knew rest would be shallow and waking inevitable.

That night, the sensation did not fade.

She lay still, listening to the house settle. Corridors quieted. Lamps dimmed. Somewhere distant, a door closed gently. The estate moved toward rest with practiced ease. Manasa did not follow.

She closed her eyes.

The lake appeared immediately.

It was not the lake as she saw it by day, framed by trees and softened by mist. This version was closer, intimate, as if she stood at its edge without distance to protect her. The water was still, reflecting nothing. The sky above it was blank, without stars or cloud.

Manasa felt no fear.

Fear came later.

She stepped forward, though her body remained motionless on the bed. The water did not ripple beneath her approach. It remained undisturbed, its surface smooth and expectant.

She knew then that the dream had chosen its form.

A sound emerged, not from the water but from within it. Not a splash or movement. A low pressure, as if the lake itself were holding breath.

Manasa waited.

From the center of the water, a circle formed. It expanded slowly, evenly, with deliberate patience. Each widening ring carried weight, pressing outward, altering nothing yet promising consequence.

Faces appeared within the reflection.

They were not clear at first. Shapes formed and dissolved. Features aligned briefly before slipping away. Manasa recognized none of them, yet familiarity clung to the vision.

These were not strangers.

They were **unacknowledged**.

A sensation moved through her then, sharp and sudden. Grief without origin. Guilt without ownership. The emotions did not belong to her, yet they passed through her with clarity.

She understood.

This was not memory.

This was **inevitability**.

The dream shifted.

The lake receded, replaced by corridors that extended beyond sight. Walls rose on either side, their surfaces smooth and unmarked. Doors lined the passage, identical and closed. The air felt heavy, resistant.

Manasa walked forward.

She did not choose a door. She did not need to.

One opened on its own.

Inside, the room was empty. No furniture. No objects. Only a single figure standing at the center.

The figure faced away from her.

She did not need to see the face to know who it was.

Jaya Lakshmi.

The woman stood rigid, her posture controlled but strained. Her hands were clenched at her sides. The air around her felt dense, charged with restrained emotion.

Manasa tried to speak.

No sound emerged.

The figure turned slowly.

The face was calm. Too calm. Eyes steady. Lips neutral.

Yet something was wrong.

The eyes did not reflect the room.

They reflected the lake.

The water moved again, faster now. Circles overlapped. Pressure increased. The sound returned, louder, insistent.

Manasa felt pain then. Not physical. Emotional weight pressed against her chest, constricting breath. The sensation was unbearable, yet she did not resist it.

She had learned not to.

The figure took a step forward.

Then another.

With each step, the room darkened. The walls receded. The corridor vanished.

Only the lake remained.

And then the water broke.

Not violently. Not suddenly.

It parted.

From beneath the surface, something rose.

Not a body.

Not a shape.

A **truth**.

It had no form, yet it occupied space. It pressed outward, demanding acknowledgment. The pressure grew until Manasa felt she might fracture beneath it.

She woke with a sharp intake of breath.

The room was dark. The air felt thick. Her heart beat rapidly but steadily. She sat upright, pressing a hand against her chest.

The dream lingered.

Not as image, but as weight.

Manasa did not cry. Tears would have offered release. This sensation allowed none.

She rose quietly and moved toward the window. Outside, the lake lay still beneath the night sky. Moonlight traced its surface faintly. Nothing stirred.

Yet she knew.

The dream had not been symbolic.

It had been **directional**.

She wrapped a shawl around herself and stepped into the corridor. The house was silent, but silence here carried awareness. She moved carefully, her steps light.

She did not intend to find anyone.

She intended to understand.

The central hall was dimly lit, the painting barely visible in the low light. Manasa stopped at the entrance, unwilling to cross the threshold.

The painting drew attention even without clarity.

She felt it then, a sharp sensation behind her eyes.

Not pain.

Recognition.

Manasa turned away.

She did not approach the painting.

She walked instead toward Ajay's room.

She paused outside his door, uncertain. He had not asked to be involved in her dreams. He had not invited explanation.

Yet the dream had not belonged to her alone.

She knocked softly.

The door opened almost immediately.

Ajay stood there, fully awake.

"You felt it," she said.

"Yes," he replied.

They did not explain further.

She entered and sat on the edge of the chair opposite his bed. Her hands trembled slightly. Ajay noticed but did not comment.

"It has started," she said.

"What has" Ajay asked.

She closed her eyes briefly.

"The sequence," she said. "The order of things."

Ajay waited.

"I do not see events," she continued. "I feel outcomes. I feel weight before it falls."

"Yes."

"The lake showed me something tonight," she said. "Not what will happen. Who will be unable to escape it."

Ajay remained silent.

"Do you believe dreams lie" she asked.

"No," Ajay said. "They reveal without responsibility."

She nodded.

"This one did not offer comfort," she said. "It offered clarity."

"Clarity is rarely gentle," Ajay replied.

She looked at him then, truly looked.

"You are not afraid," she said.

"No."

"Why"

"Because I am not required to choose," Ajay said. "Only to witness."

She considered this.

"I am not given that distance," she said.

"No," Ajay agreed. "You are closer to the weight."

Silence settled between them.

"The painting," she said quietly. "It is not the cause."

"No," Ajay replied. "It is the mirror."

She exhaled slowly.

"Then the house," she said. "The land. The lake."

"They are participants," Ajay said. "Not initiators."

She stood.

"I will dream again," she said. "Soon."

"Yes."

"And when I do," she added, "someone will move closer to consequence."

"Yes."

She left without another word.

Ajay sat alone in the dim room, aware of the subtle shift in the estate. Something had crossed a threshold that could not be undone.

The first dream had arrived.

Not as warning.

As **announcement**.

Outside, the lake remained still.

But beneath its surface, movement had begun.

# CHAPTER NINE

# THE HALL OF ANCESTORS

Morning entered the central hall cautiously, as if aware that the space required permission. Light filtered through the tall windows in narrow bands, illuminating portions of the floor while leaving the ceiling untouched. Shadows gathered near the corners, where memory seemed to prefer stillness.

Ajay arrived early.

He did not come with purpose. Purpose implied intention. He came because the hall had begun to insist upon presence. Since the painting had been placed, the space no longer behaved as it once had. Sound lingered differently. Distance compressed. Silence thickened.

The portraits watched.

They always had.

But now their presence felt sharpened, as if observation had shifted from passive to deliberate.

Ajay walked slowly along the walls, studying the faces without assigning judgment. Men and women from different eras stared outward, expressions carefully composed. Authority rested heavily in their eyes. Control had been practiced here long before it had been inherited.

He stopped before a portrait positioned closest to the painting.

The man depicted there was older than the others, his features carved by restraint rather than indulgence. His eyes held a steadiness that resisted interpretation. Ajay felt the familiar internal pressure rise.

Not discomfort.

Recognition.

This man had understood consequence.

Ajay turned toward the painting.

It occupied its space without arrogance. The canvas neither dominated nor receded. It simply existed, reflecting without distortion. Light fell unevenly across its surface, revealing details slowly, as if rewarding patience.

The figure within the painting stood beside water.

Not reaching for it.

Not retreating.

Waiting.

Ajay sensed movement behind him.

Jaya Lakshmi entered the hall without announcement. Her presence altered the air immediately. Authority settled like weight, pressing downward.

"You spend time here," she said.

"Yes," Ajay replied.

"This hall is not for reflection," she said. "It is for remembrance."

"Remembrance is reflection," Ajay replied.

She did not respond immediately.

"You look at them as if they might speak," she said, gesturing toward the portraits.

"They already have," Ajay said. "Through what remains."

She stepped closer.

"These people built this estate," she said. "Their decisions shaped everything you see."

"Yes."

"They made sacrifices," she continued. "They endured loss."

"Yes."

"They were not gentle," she said.

"No."

Silence followed.

"You believe the past demands something," she said.

"The past demands acknowledgment," Ajay replied. "Not submission."

She turned toward the painting.

"This one unsettles you," she said.

"No," Ajay replied. "It unsettles what has been protected."

Her jaw tightened.

"Protection is not concealment," she said.

"Protection often begins there," Ajay replied.

She faced him.

"You imply wrongdoing," she said.

"I imply **unresolved** action," Ajay replied.

She stared at him for a long moment.

"This hall," she said finally, "has witnessed death."

Ajay did not react.

"Deaths are not uncommon in old houses," she continued. "Illness. Accidents. Time."

"Yes."

"But you believe something else," she said.

"I believe patterns remain visible," Ajay replied. "Even when events are separated by years."

Her expression hardened.

"You were not here then," she said.

"No," Ajay replied. "But the hall was."

She turned away.

"You speak as if walls remember," she said.

"They do," Ajay replied. "They absorb what people refuse to carry."

Jaya Lakshmi walked toward the far end of the hall, stopping beneath a cluster of portraits.

"These are my ancestors," she said. "They did what was necessary."

"Yes."

"You judge necessity easily," she said.

"No," Ajay replied. "I observe consequence."

She inhaled slowly.

"Consequence," she repeated. "A convenient word."

"It arrives regardless of convenience," Ajay replied.

The sound of footsteps interrupted them.

Manasa entered quietly, stopping near the entrance. Her presence felt lighter, yet more vulnerable. Her eyes moved immediately to the painting.

She did not approach.

"You should not be here," Jaya Lakshmi said.

"I was called," Manasa replied softly.

"By whom"

Manasa hesitated.

"The hall," she said.

Jaya Lakshmi frowned.

"This is not a place for imagination," she said.

Manasa looked toward Ajay briefly.

"I did not imagine it," she said. "I felt it."

Ajay remained silent.

"What did you feel" Jaya Lakshmi asked.

Manasa swallowed.

"Pressure," she said. "Weight."

"Dreams," Jaya Lakshmi dismissed. "They distort."

"Not always," Ajay said.

Jaya Lakshmi turned sharply toward him.

"You encourage this," she said.

"I acknowledge it," Ajay replied.

Manasa stepped closer to the painting, though she stopped several steps away.

"It is not the cause," she said quietly. "It is the surface."

Jaya Lakshmi laughed softly.

"Surfaces do not kill," she said.

"No," Manasa replied. "They reveal."

Silence settled heavily.

The hall responded.

Light shifted subtly, altering the expressions within the portraits. Shadows deepened near the ceiling. The air thickened, pressing inward.

Jaya Lakshmi felt it.

She straightened.

"This conversation ends here," she said. "You will both return to your duties."

She turned and left the hall.

Manasa remained still for a moment longer.

"She knows," she said quietly.

"Partially," Ajay replied. "Enough to resist."

"That makes it worse," Manasa said.

"Yes," Ajay agreed.

They stood in silence.

"The hall is awake now," Manasa said.

"It always was," Ajay replied. "Awareness has shifted."

She looked at the portraits again.

"They are not watching us," she said. "They are watching her."

"Yes."

"What happens next" she asked.

Ajay considered the question.

"The past seeks audience," he said. "When denied, it raises its voice."

Manasa shuddered slightly.

"I will dream again," she said.

"Yes."

"And when I do," she added, "the hall will not remain neutral."

"No," Ajay replied. "It never truly was."

She left quietly.

Ajay remained alone with the portraits and the painting.

The hall felt altered now.

Not hostile.

Attentive.

The ancestors had been invoked, not by ritual or intent, but by recognition. What had been buried beneath **control** had shifted closer to surface.

The hall had accepted its role.And once memory chose to speak, silence could no longer protect those who had relied upon it.

# CHAPTER TEN

# THE MYTH THAT WAITS

The painting did not announce its history. It did not demand interpretation or invite discussion. It remained still within the central hall, accepting light and shadow with equal restraint. Its presence altered the space without altering itself.

Ajay understood that restraint immediately.

Myths that survived centuries did so not because they were loud, but because they were **patient**.

He returned to the hall alone that afternoon, drawn not by curiosity but by alignment. The house felt quieter now, though activity continued elsewhere. Footsteps moved along distant corridors. Voices rose briefly and settled. The hall remained untouched by that movement, as if it existed in a separate layer of time.

Ajay stood before the painting and allowed his attention to rest without direction.

The figure beside the water appeared unchanged, yet something within the image had shifted since the previous day. The stillness felt deeper. The water darker. The reflection less forgiving.

He noticed details he had not examined before.

The figure's posture was not tense. It was resigned. Not defeated, but accepting of consequence. The water beside him reflected more than his form. It carried impressions of others, shapes just beneath the surface, present without clarity.

Ajay felt the internal pressure rise again.

Not discomfort.

Recognition.

This was not a story of punishment.

It was a story of **choice**.

The myth did not begin with violence. It began with denial.

Ajay closed his eyes briefly and allowed memory to surface.

The collector had spoken once, during a long conversation Ajay had dismissed as irrelevant at the time. The man had traced the painting's origin with care, his voice reverent but precise.

"It is a lesser known version," the collector had said. "Not the popular telling. Not the one where justice arrives with spectacle."

Ajay remembered nodding without interest.

Now the words returned with clarity.

The myth spoke of a man who had committed no visible crime. He had not struck a blow. He had not spilled blood. He had merely allowed injustice to continue because intervention threatened comfort.

The water beside him in the painting represented memory. Not memory of what had happened, but memory of what had been **avoided**.

The figure waited.

Not for forgiveness.

For acknowledgment.

Ajay opened his eyes.

The painting did not accuse.

It reflected.

That was its power.

He sensed presence behind him.

Manasa stood at the edge of the hall, her posture tense but controlled. She did not approach closer.

"You see it now," she said.

"Yes," Ajay replied.

"It does not frighten you," she said.

"No."

"It frightens me," she said.

"Because you feel its direction," Ajay replied.

She nodded.

"It does not show what was done," she said. "It shows what will not remain buried."

"Yes."

She took a tentative step forward, then stopped.

"I dreamed again," she said.

"When"

"Before dawn," she replied. "The water moved faster."

Ajay remained silent.

"The faces were clearer," she continued. "Not names. Not features. Intention."

"Whose" Ajay asked.

She hesitated.

"Those who benefited," she said.

Ajay looked at the painting again.

"The myth never punished the man directly," he said. "It punished the structure that allowed him to remain untouched."

Manasa shuddered slightly.

"That structure is alive here," she said.

"Yes."

They stood together in silence, facing the canvas.

Footsteps echoed briefly in the corridor.

Jaya Lakshmi entered.

She did not look at either of them at first. Her gaze moved immediately to the painting. Her posture was composed, but effort was visible now. Control required maintenance.

"You stand before it often," she said.

"Yes," Ajay replied.

"You allow it to influence you," she said.

"No," Ajay replied. "It allows influence to surface."

She turned sharply toward him.

"You speak as if it were conscious," she said.

"Consciousness is not required," Ajay replied. "Alignment is."

She looked back at the painting.

"I do not like myths," she said. "They encourage moral confusion."

"They encourage memory," Ajay replied.

"Memory is selective," she said.

"Yes," Ajay agreed. "That is why myths persist. They preserve what selection discards."

She stepped closer to the painting than she ever had before.

Up close, the details became unavoidable. The cracks in the varnish. The deepened tones where time had settled. The water's surface appeared almost textured, as if movement had been frozen mid breath.

She stared.

"This man," she said slowly, "did nothing."

"Yes," Ajay replied.

"And yet he suffers," she said.

"He waits," Ajay corrected.

"For what" she asked.

"For himself," Ajay replied.

She turned away abruptly.

"You speak in riddles," she said.

"I speak in reflections," Ajay replied.

Manasa shifted uncomfortably.

"You should not be here," Jaya Lakshmi said to her.

"I know," Manasa replied. "But it called."

Jaya Lakshmi laughed softly.

"Paintings do not call," she said.

"No," Manasa replied. "Memory does."

Silence followed.

The hall responded.

Light shifted again, dimming slightly as clouds passed outside. Shadows deepened near the portraits. The air thickened, pressing inward with subtle insistence.

Jaya Lakshmi inhaled slowly.

"This ends now," she said. "The painting will be moved."

Ajay did not react.

Manasa looked toward him briefly.

"Where" Manasa asked.

"Anywhere but here," Jaya Lakshmi replied.

Ajay spoke calmly.

"It will not change what has aligned," he said.

She turned on him.

"You assume too much," she said.

"No," Ajay replied. "I observe consequence."

Her eyes hardened.

"You were not invited to interpret our past," she said.

"No," Ajay replied. "I was invited to witness its arrival."

She stared at him, then looked away.

"Leave," she said to both of them.

They did.

That night, the painting remained in the hall.

No one touched it.

The house seemed to hold breath.

Manasa did not sleep. She sat near her window, listening to the lake respond to something unseen. The water moved faintly, though no wind disturbed it.

Ajay remained awake as well.

He did not think.

He listened.

Something had shifted within Jaya Lakshmi.

Resistance had surfaced.

Resistance always preceded collapse.

The myth had not demanded belief.

It had demanded **recognition**.

And recognition, once denied, did not retreat.

It waited.

# CHAPTER ELEVEN

# THE THING THAT REFUSES TO LEAVE

The decision to move the painting was spoken once and never repeated.

Jaya Lakshmi did not announce it publicly. She did not summon staff or issue instructions that might invite discussion. Authority, when exercised correctly, did not explain itself. It assumed compliance.

Yet the painting remained.

Morning arrived without disturbance. The house followed routine. Meals were prepared. Corridors were cleaned. Supervisors reported as usual. The central hall stood exactly as it had the night before.

The painting occupied its place against the wall.

No one admitted noticing.

Denial required collective effort.

Ajay arrived in the hall shortly after sunrise. He did not expect to find the painting gone. Expectation implied desire. He observed.

Light entered cautiously, settling first upon the floor, then climbing the wall until it reached the canvas. The figure beside the water appeared unchanged. The stillness remained intact.

Ajay felt the internal pressure rise.

Not discomfort.

Alignment.

The painting was not resisting removal.

It simply had not been moved.

He turned at the sound of footsteps.

Jaya Lakshmi entered the hall with measured composure. Her expression was neutral, her posture controlled. If she felt anything, it did not surface easily.

She stopped several steps from the painting.

"You are here early," she said.

"Yes."

She did not comment further.

Her gaze moved slowly from the canvas to the portraits, then to the far windows. She did not look directly at the painting again.

"It should not still be here," she said, not as accusation but as statement.

"No," Ajay replied.

She turned sharply toward him.

"You were told it would be moved," she said.

"Yes."

"And yet it remains," she said.

"Yes."

She inhaled slowly.

"Do you know why" she asked.

"Yes," Ajay replied.

She waited.

"Because it has been **accepted**," he said.

Her jaw tightened.

"By whom" she asked.

"By the house," Ajay replied.

She laughed softly.

"You speak as if walls decide," she said.

"They respond," Ajay replied. "Decision follows response."

She looked away.

"I gave instructions," she said. "They were clear."

"Yes."

"Then why" she asked.

"Because compliance cannot override alignment," Ajay said.

She stared at the painting now, unwillingly.

"It is an object," she said. "Objects do not possess will."

"No," Ajay replied. "They possess meaning."

She stepped closer, stopping just short of the canvas.

Up close, the details asserted themselves. The cracks in the surface. The deepened shadows near the water. The figure's stillness appeared heavier now, less passive.

Jaya Lakshmi felt it.

She stepped back abruptly.

"This is absurd," she said. "A coincidence."

"Yes," Ajay replied. "Until repetition."

Her gaze hardened.

"You believe repetition has begun," she said.

"Yes."

She turned away.

The hall responded subtly. Sound shifted. Distance compressed. Silence thickened.

Jaya Lakshmi moved toward the far end of the hall, her steps measured but tense.

"Summon the staff," she said.

"Yes," Ajay replied.

When the staff arrived, they stood near the entrance, their posture attentive but uncertain. Jaya Lakshmi gestured toward the painting.

"This will be moved," she said.

No one moved.

The hesitation was brief but undeniable.

Ajay watched carefully.

"Is there a problem" she asked sharply.

One of the older attendants spoke, his voice low.

"Madam," he said, "the frame does not lift easily."

Jaya Lakshmi frowned.

"Then try again," she said.

Two men approached the painting. They grasped the frame carefully, applying steady pressure. The canvas did not budge.

They adjusted their grip and tried again.

Nothing.

The painting remained fixed, not by force, but by refusal.

The men stepped back, unsettled.

Jaya Lakshmi stared.

"This is impossible," she said.

"No," Ajay replied. "It is **inertia**."

She turned toward him.

"You arranged this," she accused.

"No," Ajay replied calmly. "I observed it."

She raised her voice slightly.

"Remove it," she said.

The men tried once more.

The frame resisted without effort.

No sound emerged. No crack. No indication of obstruction.

The painting simply remained.

Silence spread through the hall.

Jaya Lakshmi's control faltered briefly. Ajay noticed the shift. Her breathing altered. Her posture stiffened.

"Leave," she said sharply.

The staff withdrew quickly.

The hall returned to quiet.

Jaya Lakshmi stood alone with Ajay and the painting.

"This is manipulation," she said.

"No," Ajay replied. "This is **exposure**."

She turned away from the canvas, pacing slowly.

"You speak as if something unseen is acting," she said.

"Yes."

"And you believe this is justified," she said.

"I believe it is inevitable," Ajay replied.

She stopped.

"I will not allow this," she said.

"No one has asked permission," Ajay replied.

She looked at him with open hostility now.

"You were brought here to manage," she said. "Not to destabilize."

"Yes," Ajay replied. "Stability built on avoidance cannot be maintained."

She laughed harshly.

"You sound like a moralist," she said.

"No," Ajay replied. "I sound like a witness."

That word landed heavily.

Witness.

Jaya Lakshmi looked away.

From the doorway, Manasa observed quietly.

She had not entered. She stood at the threshold, her presence tentative but unavoidable.

"You feel it too," Jaya Lakshmi said without turning.

Manasa hesitated.

"Yes," she replied.

"What do you feel" Jaya Lakshmi asked.

Manasa swallowed.

"Pressure," she said. "Movement beneath stillness."

Jaya Lakshmi closed her eyes briefly.

"This ends today," she said. "The painting will be covered."

She gestured sharply.

An attendant returned with a cloth.

They approached cautiously and draped it over the canvas.

For a moment, nothing happened.

Then the air shifted.

Not violently. Not visibly.

Sound dulled.

Distance lengthened.

The hall felt wrong.

Manasa gasped softly.

"Do not," she said.

Jaya Lakshmi ignored her.

The cloth settled fully over the painting.

The figure disappeared.

The hall reacted.

A sharp sound echoed from somewhere above, like wood adjusting under strain. Dust fell lightly from a beam. The portraits seemed to darken, their expressions tightening.

Jaya Lakshmi stepped back.

"What is this" she whispered.

"**Resistance**," Ajay replied. "It increases pressure."

She stared at the covered painting.

"Remove it," she said.

The attendant hesitated, then pulled the cloth away.

The moment the canvas was revealed, the hall exhaled.

Sound returned.

Distance corrected.

Stillness resumed.

Manasa steadied herself.

"It does not tolerate concealment," she said.

Ajay nodded.

"It does not punish," he said. "It responds."

Jaya Lakshmi's composure cracked slightly.

"This house obeys me," she said, though uncertainty edged her voice.

"It remembers you," Ajay replied.

She turned toward him, her eyes sharp with something close to fear.

"You will leave," she said suddenly. "Soon."

"Yes," Ajay replied. "When observation is complete."

She looked at the painting again.

Observation had begun long before his arrival.

That night, the first **physical** consequence occurred.

A worker from the gardens was found unconscious near the lake. Not injured. Not ill. Simply unresponsive.

Manasa felt it before she was told.

Ajay sensed it without being informed.

Jaya Lakshmi stood in the hall, staring at the painting long after midnight.

The thing that refused to leave had done more than remain.

It had **anchored** itself.

And from anchoring came inevitability.

# CHAPTER TWELVE

## WHAT THE PAST ALLOWS

Ajay did not collapse when the vision arrived.

There was no dizziness, no sudden intrusion, no sense of invasion. The transition occurred quietly, as if the boundary between present and past had thinned on its own. One moment he stood in the corridor outside the central hall, the next he stood somewhere else entirely.

The shift was not visual at first.

It was **weight**.

Pressure gathered behind his eyes and along his chest, not painful but insistent. His breath slowed without instruction. Sound receded. The estate did not disappear. It layered.

Ajay understood immediately that this was not imagination.

Imagination required participation.

This did not.

The corridor remained around him, yet something else existed beneath it, aligned but displaced. He felt the texture of time change, like fabric turned inside out.

Then the images arrived.

The tea gardens appeared first.

Not as they were now, trimmed and disciplined, but uneven and raw. The plants were taller, less restrained. The paths were narrower. Workers moved with urgency rather than routine. Voices carried tension instead of habit.

Ajay stood unseen among them.

A man walked ahead, his posture rigid, his steps purposeful. He wore simple clothes stained with soil and sweat. His hands were rough, his movements direct. He carried responsibility without authority.

The land recognized him.

Ajay felt it.

This man belonged to the gardens in a way ownership never achieved.

The vision shifted.

A meeting took place near the edge of the estate. Several figures stood together, their expressions guarded. Among them was a younger Jaya Lakshmi. Her posture was straighter then, her gaze sharper, less practiced in restraint.

Another man stood opposite her.

Her husband.

He spoke calmly, his tone measured, his words chosen carefully. He held documents in his hand, papers that represented division, allocation, inheritance.

Ajay did not hear every word.

He did not need to.

The tension lay not in speech, but in what remained unsaid.

The man from the gardens stood nearby, listening.

He was not meant to be present.

Yet he was.

The younger Jaya Lakshmi noticed him.

Her gaze lingered for a fraction longer than necessary. Something moved behind her eyes. Calculation. Comparison.

The land shifted beneath Ajay's awareness.

The vision deepened.

Time moved forward without transition.

The man from the gardens now stood alone near the lake. His posture had changed. The confidence that once anchored him had eroded. His shoulders slumped. His gaze darted occasionally toward the bungalow, then away.

Ajay felt the pressure increase.

Something had already happened.

The vision sharpened.

The man was accused.

Not publicly. Quietly. Through suggestion rather than declaration. A theft implied. A boundary crossed. Responsibility displaced.

No evidence surfaced.

None was required.

The accusation did not need truth. It needed **acceptance**.

Ajay felt the injustice settle like sediment.

The man protested.

Not loudly.

With confusion.

He spoke of years of labor. Of loyalty. Of land he had nurtured without claim.

His words dissolved before they reached anyone willing to hear them.

The younger Jaya Lakshmi watched.

She did not intervene.

Intervention threatened comfort.

Ajay felt something break.

Not suddenly.

Gradually.

The vision moved again.

The man was dismissed.

Not formally.

He was reassigned. Reduced. Removed from visibility.

He walked the estate as a shadow of his former presence. Workers avoided his gaze, not out of cruelty but fear. Association carried risk.

The lake appeared again.

Still.

Patient.

The man stood at its edge one evening as light faded. He did not intend to step into it. He did not consider death.

He considered escape.

Escape required decision.

The decision did not arrive.

Instead, something else occurred.

Voices approached.

Two figures emerged from the shadows.

Not strangers.

Men who benefited from his removal.

They spoke calmly.

They offered explanation without apology.

They spoke of necessity.

Of protection.

Of order.

Ajay felt the weight press harder.

The man's protests rose briefly, then faded. He realized something crucial in that moment.

He had already been erased.

What followed was not violence.

It was neglect.

The man fell.

Not pushed.

Allowed.

The lake accepted him without sound.

Ajay felt the water close over memory.

The vision shifted abruptly.

The younger Jaya Lakshmi stood in the central hall.

Her expression was composed.

News arrived quietly.

An accident.

A tragedy.

Unfortunate.

She listened.

She nodded.

She did not ask questions.

The house absorbed the event.

The land adjusted.

Time moved forward.

The gardens grew orderly.

Profits increased.

Silence stabilized.

Ajay felt the weight peak.

Then the vision began to release.

The images softened.

Edges blurred.

The corridor returned.

Ajay stood exactly where he had been.

His breath remained steady.

His heart rate unchanged.

Only awareness had altered.

He leaned against the wall briefly, not from weakness but alignment.

This was the first truth.

Not the only one.

The estate had not punished.

It had waited.

Ajay straightened and walked toward the hall.

Inside, Jaya Lakshmi stood before the painting.

She turned as he entered.

"You look pale," she said.

"No," Ajay replied. "Clear."

She studied him carefully.

"You saw something," she said.

"Yes."

She did not ask what.

She did not need to.

"Memory lies," she said quietly.

"No," Ajay replied. "It accumulates."

She turned back to the painting.

"You believe this," she said.

"I witnessed it," Ajay replied.

Her shoulders stiffened.

"You will not speak of this," she said.

"No," Ajay replied. "I will observe what follows."

She laughed softly.

"You think the past can reach forward," she said.

"It already has," Ajay replied.

Silence settled heavily.

That night, Manasa dreamed again.

This time, the lake did not remain still.

Ripples spread rapidly.

The face of the man surfaced briefly before dissolving.

Manasa woke with tears she did not understand.

The injustice had been allowed once.

Allowance did not expire.

It compounded.

Ajay stood near the window of his room, looking out toward the darkened gardens.

The past had not returned seeking revenge.

It had returned seeking **completion**.

And completion, once initiated, did not retreat.

## CHAPTER FOURTEEN

## THE DREAM OF BLOOD

Manasa understood, even before sleep touched her, that this dream would not be symbolic.

Symbols offered distance. They softened meaning and disguised direction. What approached her that night carried no such courtesy. It arrived with **clarity**, pressing against awareness long before her body surrendered to rest.

She lay still on the bed, eyes open, breath slow, listening to the estate settle. The house no longer lulled its occupants into false comfort. It moved carefully now, as if conscious of its own memory. Doors closed softly. Footsteps withdrew early. Silence arrived sooner than expected.

Outside her window, the lake reflected nothing.

No moonlight touched it. No breeze disturbed its surface. It existed as a dark plane, waiting.

Manasa turned away from the window and closed her eyes.

The dream did not build gradually. It took her whole.

She stood at the edge of the lake, closer than she had ever been while awake. The water lay unnaturally still, thick as polished stone. The air around her felt dense, resistant, as if breathing itself required permission.

She looked down.

Her reflection did not appear.

Instead, the surface showed movement beneath. Shapes formed and dissolved, not as images but as **intentions**. The water held weight, not depth. It pressed upward, insisting on recognition.

Manasa felt it then. The first trace of **blood**.

Not a sight. Not a wound. A presence.

The sensation moved through her chest sharply, constricting breath. Her heart responded instinctively, quickening despite her stillness. She did not resist. Resistance only amplified what sought passage.

The water shifted.

A single ripple formed at the center of the lake, spreading outward in perfect symmetry. The motion was precise, deliberate. Each widening circle carried consequence, altering the surface without breaking it.

Manasa knew what this meant.

This was not warning.

This was **sequence**.

The dream shifted abruptly.

She stood now within the central hall. The ceiling loomed higher than memory allowed. Portraits lined the walls, darker than before, their expressions tightened into something closer to expectancy. The painting stood uncovered, its surface luminous despite the dim light.

The figure within it no longer waited.

It watched.

Manasa felt her feet move forward without decision. The floor beneath her seemed to soften, absorbing weight as if reluctant to release it. Each step felt measured, allowed rather than chosen.

She stopped several paces from the painting.

The water within the canvas moved.

Not visibly.

Internally.

She sensed it as pressure behind her eyes, a tightening that refused relief. Her vision blurred briefly, then sharpened.

Blood appeared.

Not flowing. Not spilled.

Contained.

It stained the water beneath the painted surface, darkening it without movement. The blood did not rise. It did not sink. It remained suspended, a memory unwilling to dissolve.

Manasa's breath caught.

This was not metaphor.

This was **inheritance**.

The hall darkened further. Light withdrew from the corners, collapsing inward. The portraits leaned subtly, their frames creaking under unseen strain.

A sound emerged.

Not footsteps.

A heartbeat.

Slow. Heavy. Deliberate.

It echoed through the hall, aligning with her own. Each beat pressed against her chest, demanding synchronization.

She felt the first death before she saw it.

A sharp compression behind the sternum. A sudden loss of warmth. A narrowing of possibility.

The dream shifted again.

She stood now in the tea gardens.

Not as they were today.

As they had been years ago.

The rows were uneven. The soil darker. The air heavier with effort rather than routine. Workers moved with urgency, their expressions strained.

One man stood apart.

His posture was familiar now. His presence carried the same weight she had felt in the lake, in the hall, in the painting. He belonged to the land in a way ownership never achieved.

Manasa watched him walk.

His steps were steady, his gaze forward, yet something had already been withdrawn from him. Authority had been removed quietly, without confrontation. Dignity eroded through **exclusion**.

She felt his confusion as if it were her own.

The dream accelerated.

Time folded.

The man stood again at the lake.

This time, she saw his face clearly.

Not fear.

Resignation.

He did not step forward.

He was not pushed.

He was **allowed to fall**.

The water closed over him without sound.

Manasa cried out then.

Her voice broke free.

The dream did not end.

Blood bloomed beneath the surface, spreading slowly, staining memory rather than water. The lake absorbed it without resistance.

The dream shifted once more.

She stood in the present.

Near the same lake.

But now someone else occupied the space.

A living man.

A worker.

His posture mirrored the one before him, though he did not yet know it. His breath came unevenly. His hand pressed against his chest as if searching for something that had already left.

Manasa felt the **alignment** lock into place.

Past and present converged.

This death would not look like punishment.

It would look like coincidence.

The worker stumbled.

Not dramatically.

His knees buckled.

He fell sideways onto the damp soil near the lake's edge.

No one was there yet.

The dream lingered on his stillness.

Blood did not spill.

It was not required.

The water stirred slightly.

Manasa felt herself being pulled backward.

The dream released her.

She woke with a gasp, sitting upright in bed, heart pounding violently. Her breath came in short bursts, chest tight, limbs trembling.

Tears streamed down her face before she understood why.

Not grief.

Recognition.

She rose quickly and crossed to the window.

Outside, the lake remained dark and still.

But something had changed.

She could feel it.

The estate had accepted the next step.

Manasa wrapped a shawl around herself and stepped into the corridor. The house was silent, yet alert. The walls seemed closer now, the air heavier.

She did not hesitate.

She walked toward Ajay's room.

She knocked once.

The door opened immediately.

Ajay stood fully awake.

"It is closer," she said.

"Yes," he replied.

"This one will not be hidden," she said. "It will happen near the lake."

Ajay nodded.

"You saw blood," he said.

"Yes."

"Not spilled," he added.

"No," she said. "Inherited."

She sat heavily in the chair, pressing her hands together to steady them.

"I did not see violence," she said. "I saw permission."

Ajay remained silent.

"That frightens me more," she said.

"Yes," he replied. "Because it removes intention."

She looked up at him.

"Can it be stopped" she asked.

Ajay met her gaze calmly.

"No," he said. "Only understood."

She closed her eyes.

"When" she asked.

"Soon," Ajay replied.

Manasa stood abruptly.

“I must go to the lake,” she said.

“No,” Ajay said gently. “You are not meant to intervene.”

She turned back to him, anger flashing briefly through fear.

“Then what is my role” she asked.

“To feel what others refuse to feel,” Ajay replied. “And to survive it.”

Her shoulders sagged.

“That feels like punishment,” she said.

“No,” Ajay replied. “It is **witness**.”

She left without another word.

Morning arrived with unnatural stillness.

The estate woke slowly, as if reluctant.

Workers gathered later than usual. Conversation remained minimal. The air near the lake felt heavier, charged.

Before noon, the news spread quietly.

A worker had collapsed near the lake.

He was alive when found.

Barely.

By evening, he was dead.

The doctors spoke of cardiac failure. Of stress. Of heat. Of coincidence.

Jaya Lakshmi accepted the explanation with rigid composure.

Ajay stood near the lake that night, watching the water return to stillness.

Manasa did not approach.

She could not.

The dream had been fulfilled.

Not as vengeance.

As **completion**.

The first present death had aligned with the past.

And now the sequence had proven itself.

There would be no retreat.

Only continuation.

## CHAPTER FIFTEEN

## THE SHAPE OF INJUSTICE

The estate did not mourn.

It adjusted.

Ajay noticed this first in the gardens. Work resumed with minimal delay, as if routine itself were a form of containment. Leaves were plucked. Baskets were filled. Paths were walked in familiar sequence. The land absorbed the absence of one body without altering its rhythm.

Human grief was loud.

Land responded with **continuity**.

Ajay stood at the edge of the lake as morning unfolded. The water reflected the pale sky without distortion. Nothing on its surface suggested that a life had ended there hours earlier. No ripple lingered. No trace remained.

That absence disturbed him more than spectacle would have.

He turned away slowly and walked back toward the bungalow. With each step, the internal pressure he had come to recognize deepened. It did not overwhelm him. It aligned him.

The second vision arrived before he reached the corridor.

This one did not pull him away from the present.

It overlaid it.

The gardens remained before him, but something beneath them stirred. Ajay felt the texture of time shift again, thinner now, more permeable.

He stopped walking.

Workers passed him without noticing.

The estate had begun to use him as a **conduit**.

Images surfaced.

Not scenes.

Structures.

He saw transactions without words. Decisions made quietly. Papers signed in rooms where no witnesses were invited. Power exercised not through command, but through omission.

The brother appeared.

Not as a villain.

As a man who had failed himself.

Ajay saw him years earlier, standing in one of the commercial buildings newly constructed at the time. His posture lacked certainty. His gaze shifted often, searching for validation.

The elder brother had inherited land.

This one inherited **freedom**.

Freedom without discipline became erosion.

Ajay felt the imbalance immediately.

The brother spent without restraint. He invested without understanding. He trusted voices that echoed his own desires. Loss accumulated gradually, disguised as opportunity.

When he returned to the estate seeking support, the response was measured.

Not refusal.

Delay.

Delay was safer.

Jaya Lakshmi appeared younger again in this layer of memory. Her expression was attentive, sympathetic, precise. She spoke of responsibility. Of consequences. Of self made outcomes.

Her words were correct.

Her timing was not.

Ajay saw how she allowed the brother's decline to continue unchecked. She did not cause it. She permitted it.

Permission did not require action.

It required silence.

The vision sharpened.

The brother stood before her once more, this time diminished. His voice trembled. His eyes carried something close to desperation.

He asked for land.

Not ownership.

Access.

The request unsettled her.

Land was permanence.

Permanence threatened comparison.

Ajay felt the familiar tightening behind his eyes.

The decision occurred quietly.

She refused.

Not openly.

She redirected.

She suggested delay.

She spoke of future reassessment.

The brother left.

The estate adjusted.

Time moved forward.

Ajay felt the weight accumulate.

The brother's decline accelerated. Debt closed in. Reputation eroded. Relationships dissolved. Each failure reinforced the narrative of self destruction.

The estate watched.

So did she.

Ajay saw her then, standing at a window overlooking the gardens, listening to news of the brother's final collapse. Her expression remained controlled, yet something dark moved beneath it.

Not satisfaction.

Relief.

Relief that comparison no longer threatened.

Relief that the land remained **unshared**.

Ajay exhaled slowly.

The vision deepened further.

Now he saw the connection clearly.

The worker who had died recently.

The man who had drowned years earlier.

The brother who had ruined himself.

Different lives.

Different choices.

One structure.

The estate rewarded alignment with its authority and eroded those who disrupted its hierarchy.

Not through violence.

Through **permission**.

Ajay leaned against the stone railing near the garden path, steadying himself.

The vision released gradually, leaving residue rather than shock.

This was not a story of cruelty.

It was a story of selective compassion.

That realization disturbed him deeply.

Selective compassion wore the mask of morality.

Jaya Lakshmi did not consider herself unjust.

She considered herself responsible.

Ajay walked toward the bungalow with measured steps. Each corridor now felt narrower, its walls closer. The house seemed to press inward, reducing distance.

He found Jaya Lakshmi in the central hall.

She stood alone, facing the portraits.

"You have been walking the estate often," she said without turning.

"Yes," Ajay replied.

"You observe too much," she said.

"Yes," Ajay agreed.

She turned toward him slowly.

"The worker's death," she said. "Doctors called it coincidence."

"Yes."

"You do not believe that," she said.

"No."

Her gaze sharpened.

"You believe the estate is punishing us," she said.

"No," Ajay replied. "It is completing itself."

She frowned.

"Completion implies design," she said.

"No," Ajay replied. "It implies accumulation."

She stepped closer.

"You speak as if the past demands resolution," she said.

"Yes."

"And you believe I am responsible," she said.

"Yes," Ajay replied. "And no."

She paused.

"Explain," she said.

"You did not cause every outcome," Ajay said. "But you **allowed** each one."

Her face tightened.

"Allowance is not action," she said.

"Allowance shapes action," Ajay replied.

She turned away abruptly.

"You misunderstand leadership," she said. "I protected what was mine."

"Yes," Ajay replied. "At the cost of others."

She faced him again, anger surfacing.

"People destroy themselves," she said. "I did not ruin my brother. I did not drown that worker. I did not stop anyone from living."

"No," Ajay replied. "You stopped them from belonging."

The words settled heavily.

Belonging.

Jaya Lakshmi inhaled sharply.

"You think belonging is owed," she said.

"No," Ajay replied. "I think denial accumulates."

She shook her head.

"You speak like a judge," she said.

"No," Ajay replied. "I speak like **memory**."

Silence stretched between them.

From the doorway, Manasa watched quietly.

She felt the tension as physical weight. Her dreams had sharpened her awareness. She sensed the pressure building within Jaya Lakshmi, the fracture beneath control.

"You are not afraid," Manasa said softly.

Jaya Lakshmi turned sharply.

"Fear is weakness," she said.

"No," Manasa replied. "Fear is **recognition**."

Jaya Lakshmi stared at her.

"You dream too much," she said.

"I feel too much," Manasa replied.

That night, the estate reacted outwardly.

A machine in one of the tea manufacturing units malfunctioned unexpectedly. Not violently. It simply stopped. Production halted briefly. Workers stood uncertain, waiting for instruction.

The pause was short.

But it was unprecedented.

Ajay stood near the factory floor, listening to the sudden absence of sound. Machines that had moved endlessly now remained still.

Silence pressed inward.

The estate had begun to resist its own rhythm.

Later, as dusk fell, Ajay walked once more to the lake.

The water reflected the fading sky with unsettling calm. He felt the pressure again, stronger now.

This was not another vision.

This was **confirmation**.

The injustice had shape now. It had pattern. It had direction.

And direction did not reverse.

Behind him, Manasa stood quietly.

"It will continue," she said.

"Yes," Ajay replied.

"How many" she asked.

"As many as memory requires," Ajay replied.

She closed her eyes.

"And her" she asked.

Ajay looked toward the bungalow.

"She will be last," he said.

Manasa shuddered.

"That feels cruel," she said.

"No," Ajay replied. "It feels precise."

The estate settled into night.

Lights dimmed unevenly. Corridors lengthened. Sound traveled farther.

Jaya Lakshmi stood alone in the central hall long after others slept.

She stared at the painting.

Not in fear.

In resistance.

Resistance tightened its grip.

And resistance always sharpened what followed.

# CHAPTER SIXTEEN

# THE BIRTH OF JEALOUSY

Jealousy did not arrive in Jaya Lakshmi's life as emotion.

It arrived as **comparison**.

This distinction mattered, though she would not have named it at the time. Emotion could be dismissed as weakness. Comparison felt rational. Necessary. A method of calibration in a world where survival depended upon knowing one's position.

From childhood, she learned to measure.

Not affection. Not morality.

Position.

Her family did not raise children. They raised successors. Each gesture was observed. Each achievement weighed. Praise was distributed sparingly, never enough to satisfy but sufficient to sharpen hunger.

Her brother was different.

He laughed more easily. Failed openly. Recovered quickly. Where Jaya Lakshmi carried expectation like armor, he wore possibility like ornament. The family indulged him not because they trusted him, but because they did not fear him.

Fear was reserved for those who appeared capable.

From early years, she learned that approval followed restraint. That love followed usefulness. That land followed obedience.

Jealousy did not feel ugly then.

It felt **justified**.

She studied harder. She listened longer. She learned silence before speech. While her brother drifted, she anchored herself into the estate's rhythms. She learned the names of plants before she learned her own desires. She memorized routes through the gardens, not to wander but to observe.

The land responded to her discipline.

This response reinforced belief.

If the land favored her, then she must deserve it.

Comparison hardened into certainty.

When her father fell ill, it was assumed she would step forward. Not because she was eldest or strongest, but because she was already present. Presence mattered more than affection.

Her brother did not contest this.

He left.

That departure carved the first fracture.

Not abandonment.

Escape.

She watched him go without protest. Protest would have implied need. Need was vulnerability. Vulnerability invited loss.

She remained.

And remaining taught her something essential.

Power arrived quietly.

It did not announce itself. It did not demand allegiance. It accumulated through routine. Each small decision compounded until it formed authority that no longer required explanation.

When she married, it was into alignment.

Her husband respected the land, but did not belong to it. He admired her discipline without understanding its cost. His affection was sincere, but sincerity did not equal comprehension.

That distance mattered.

She carried responsibility while he carried reassurance.

Reassurance dulled vigilance.

Over time, she learned not to share uncertainty. Leadership required clarity. Doubt unsettled those who depended upon structure.

So she absorbed doubt privately.

Absorption hardened into silence.

Silence hardened into control.

Jealousy waited patiently.

It did not appear when her brother failed. Failure confirmed her position. It did not appear when her husband deferred. Deference reinforced her authority.

Jealousy emerged when someone else belonged to the land more naturally than she did.

The man from the gardens.

He had no ambition. No claim. No lineage.

Yet the land responded to him.

Plants thrived where he walked. Workers listened when he spoke. Decisions aligned around him without instruction. He did not command. He **cohered**.

This disturbed her deeply.

Not because he threatened her power, but because he revealed its difference.

Her authority was imposed.

His presence was **accepted**.

Comparison sharpened.

She began to observe him more closely. Not out of suspicion. Out of curiosity masked as supervision. Each time she watched him move through the estate, she felt something shift inside her.

Not anger.

Unease.

Unease suggested inadequacy.

That could not be tolerated.

She began to rationalize.

He lacked formal authority. He operated beyond structure. His influence was informal. Informality destabilized systems.

This was not jealousy.

This was **management**.

When concerns arose, she allowed them to circulate. She did not create them. She did not suppress them. She allowed them to exist long enough to gain shape.

Allowance felt neutral.

Allowance protected her from guilt.

The man did not respond aggressively. He remained confused. Confusion eroded confidence. Confidence eroded belonging.

The land watched.

It did not intervene.

The day he disappeared into the lake, she told herself she had not chosen it.

Choice required intent.

She had allowed sequence.

Allowance felt cleaner.

Years later, when her brother returned diminished, jealousy resurfaced in subtler form.

He wanted access to the land.

Access meant comparison.

Comparison threatened narrative.

She had become the responsible one. The stabilizing force. The rightful custodian.

His return destabilized identity.

She denied him not out of cruelty, but out of preservation.

Preservation felt moral.

Preservation justified refusal.

His collapse unfolded elsewhere.

Distance absolved her.

Or so she believed.

Jealousy did not scream when he died.

It exhaled.

Relief followed.

Relief frightened her more than guilt would have.

She buried that fear under efficiency.

Years passed.

The estate prospered.

Silence stabilized.

Jealousy slept.

Until Manasa arrived.

Manasa did not threaten authority.

She threatened **certainty**.

Her sensitivity unsettled Jaya Lakshmi because it did not seek power. It revealed without intention. Dreams did not require permission. Dreams bypassed structure.

Jaya Lakshmi dismissed her at first. Intuition was undisciplined. Feelings were unreliable.

Then the painting arrived.

Then the lake stirred.

Then the worker died.

Jealousy awakened again.

This time, it did not compare people.

It compared versions of herself.

The woman who believed she protected order.

The woman revealed through consequence.

The fracture widened.

She resisted not because she denied truth, but because acceptance would collapse identity. Without the narrative of responsibility, what remained was not villainy.

It was **absence**.

Absence terrified her.

That night, she walked the estate alone.

The gardens no longer comforted her. The paths felt unfamiliar. The land that once responded to discipline now felt distant.

She stopped near the lake.

The water reflected her face faintly.

For the first time, she did not recognize it.

Jealousy had completed its transformation.

It was no longer emotion.

It was **defense**.

Defense against collapse.

Defense against recognition.

Defense against herself.

Behind her, the estate remained silent.

Not approving.

Not condemning.

Waiting.

And waiting was far worse than judgment.

# CHAPTER SEVENTEEN

# THE REFUSAL TO LOOK

Denial did not arrive in Jaya Lakshmi's mind as rejection.

It arrived as **reframing**.

She did not say the events were untrue. That would have required confrontation. She said instead that they were incomplete. Partial. Misinterpreted. In need of context only she possessed.

Context became her shelter.

She repeated this quietly to herself as she stood in the central hall before sunrise. The house was dim, its vastness softened by shadow. The portraits receded into near invisibility, their outlines present but restrained. The painting remained uncovered, though she avoided looking directly at it.

Avoidance was not weakness.

It was strategy.

She had spent a lifetime mastering strategy.

The estate had not collapsed. The gardens still produced. The factories still functioned. Orders still moved outward across borders. Money arrived. Workers reported. Life continued.

This continuity became her proof.

If wrongdoing had occurred, the estate would have reacted earlier. If injustice had truly been committed, it would have surfaced immediately. Time would not have waited decades.

Time had waited.

But she did not interpret waiting as accumulation.

She interpreted it as absolution.

Jaya Lakshmi turned away from the painting and walked the length of the hall, her footsteps echoing faintly. Each sound reminded her of space she controlled. Space responded to her presence. Doors opened when she approached. Corridors aligned themselves to her pace.

Control was still intact.

She paused near the far window overlooking the gardens. Morning mist drifted lazily above the rows, blurring distance. The land looked calm, disciplined, obedient.

She inhaled deeply.

This was reality.

Not dreams. Not visions. Not whispered interpretations.

Reality was measurable.

Reality was profitable.

Reality was obedient.

She had learned early that **truth** was rarely absolute. It bent under pressure. It yielded to repetition. Those who controlled narrative controlled memory.

Memory, she reminded herself, was unreliable.

She turned sharply as footsteps approached.

Ajay stood at the entrance to the hall, his presence quiet but unavoidable. He did not enter fully. He respected thresholds. That restraint unsettled her more than intrusion would have.

"You are awake early," she said.

"Yes," he replied.

"You spend much time here," she said.

"Yes."

She waited for explanation.

None came.

That absence irritated her.

"People mistake observation for wisdom," she said. "Seeing something does not grant authority to interpret it."

"Authority is not required," Ajay replied. "Only attention."

She scoffed softly.

"You believe attention changes outcome," she said.

"No," Ajay replied. "It changes **denial**."

The word struck her sharply.

"You assume denial," she said. "I assume responsibility."

"You assume narrative," Ajay replied. "Responsibility requires response."

Her jaw tightened.

"You speak as if I have done nothing," she said.

"No," Ajay replied. "You have done what felt necessary."

She turned to face him fully.

"And that condemns me" she asked.

"No," Ajay replied. "It defines trajectory."

She laughed then, a sound without humor.

"You speak of fate as if it were mechanical," she said.

"No," Ajay replied. "It is cumulative."

She stepped closer.

"You want confession," she said.

"No," Ajay replied. "Confession implies forgiveness."

Her eyes narrowed.

"Then what do you want" she demanded.

"I want you to **look**," Ajay replied.

She turned away abruptly.

"I will not be judged by dreams and paintings," she said.

"No one is judging," Ajay replied. "The estate is remembering."

She dismissed him with a sharp gesture.

"This conversation is over," she said.

Ajay did not argue.

He stepped back.

Denial required silence to survive.

Later that morning, Jaya Lakshmi convened a meeting with her senior supervisors. She sat at the head of the long table, posture erect, voice steady.

"The recent disruptions are coincidental," she said. "Rumors will not be tolerated."

Heads nodded.

She continued calmly.

"Operations will continue as scheduled. Any deviation must be reported immediately."

Control restored through instruction.

Or so she believed.

As the meeting concluded, she noticed something she could not dismiss.

The supervisors avoided eye contact.

Not in defiance.

In discomfort.

Discomfort unsettled her.

Fear could be corrected.

Discomfort lingered.

She dismissed them abruptly.

Once alone, she felt the pressure return.

Not from the hall.

From within.

She walked through the bungalow without destination, turning corners she had memorized years ago. The house felt subtly altered now. Corridors seemed longer. Rooms felt slightly misaligned.

She stopped before a mirror in one of the side rooms.

Her reflection stared back at her.

She looked tired.

That startled her.

Fatigue suggested vulnerability.

Vulnerability suggested exposure.

She turned away quickly.

Later that day, Manasa avoided her deliberately.

This avoidance was new.

Manasa had always been respectful, cautious, deferential.

Now she moved through the house with quiet distance.

Distance felt like judgment.

Jaya Lakshmi cornered her near the veranda.

"You have been restless," she said.

"Yes," Manasa replied softly.

"You fill your mind with unnecessary fears," Jaya Lakshmi said.

"I feel what is present," Manasa replied.

"Feeling is not knowing," Jaya Lakshmi said sharply.

"No," Manasa replied. "But it precedes it."

That unsettled her.

"You should stop listening to him," Jaya Lakshmi said.

Manasa looked up.

"He does not instruct me," she said. "He listens."

That distinction irritated Jaya Lakshmi deeply.

"Listening can be manipulation," she said.

"No," Manasa replied. "It is surrender."

The word landed heavily.

Surrender was unacceptable.

Jaya Lakshmi turned away abruptly.

That evening, she ordered the painting to be covered permanently.

Not removed.

Concealed.

Concealment allowed denial to coexist with reality.

Staff hesitated, then complied.

The cloth settled over the canvas, hiding the water, the figure, the reflection.

The hall reacted immediately.

Not dramatically.

Subtly.

Sound dulled. Air thickened. Distance stretched.

Jaya Lakshmi felt it.

Her chest tightened briefly.

She ignored it.

"I will not look," she whispered to herself.

Refusal hardened into decision.

That night, she dreamed for the first time in years.

Not symbols.

Not images.

She dreamed of walking along the lake.

Her reflection followed her steps independently.

She woke with her heart racing.

Sweat soaked her clothing.

She sat upright, breath uneven.

Dreams were for the weak.

She dressed quickly and left the room, walking into the hall.

The cloth still covered the painting.

She stood before it, staring at the concealed shape.

Her hand trembled slightly.

She clenched it into a fist.

"I will not look," she repeated.

The refusal sealed something.

From that moment forward, the estate no longer waited.

It responded.

Machines malfunctioned more frequently. Workers called in sick without cause. The lake began to ripple at night despite still air.

The house grew restless.

Denial had reached its limit.

Ajay observed quietly.

Manasa felt the pressure increase.

Jaya Lakshmi tightened control.

Control always intensified before collapse.

She had chosen not to look.

And in that choice, she had surrendered the final opportunity for **recognition**.

The trajectory was now fixed.

# CHAPTER EIGHTEEN

# THE FIRST DEATH THAT COULD NOT BE HIDDEN

The estate did not wake gently that morning.

Sound arrived unevenly, as if the land itself had lost coordination. Birds called briefly, then fell silent. Machinery started later than usual. Footsteps echoed longer through the corridors before dissolving. The air felt dense, pressing against the chest with quiet insistence.

Ajay sensed it immediately.

This was not pressure accumulating.

This was **release**.

He stood near the veranda overlooking the gardens, watching mist lift unevenly from the rows of tea plants. The land looked unchanged, yet something beneath it had shifted permanently. Memory no longer hovered. It had crossed into action.

Workers moved more slowly that day. Their gestures lacked the practiced rhythm Ajay had observed since his arrival. Baskets filled unevenly. Conversations stalled before completion. No one spoke of unease, yet it threaded through the estate like invisible wire.

Denial had ended.

Not because it had been abandoned.

Because it had become **unsustainable**.

Ajay turned away from the gardens and walked toward the central hall. The house received him differently now. Corridors felt narrower, their geometry slightly altered. Sound reflected back sooner than expected. Distance compressed.

The hall was dim.

The cloth still covered the painting.

Ajay stopped several steps away, resisting the instinct to approach. Resistance was no longer required. What needed to happen would occur without assistance.

Footsteps echoed from the far end.

Manasa entered quietly, her face pale, eyes distant.

"It will happen today," she said.

"Yes," Ajay replied.

"I feel it clearly now," she said. "Not as dream. As certainty."

Ajay did not ask for details.

Certainty did not require explanation.

"Near the gardens," she added. "Where the land dips."

Ajay nodded.

"That place remembers," he said.

She wrapped her arms around herself, as if bracing against cold.

"It is not violent," she said. "But it is final."

"Yes," Ajay replied.

They stood in silence.

The cloth covering the painting shifted slightly.

Not visibly.

Perceptually.

The hall responded.

Manasa inhaled sharply.

“It is aware,” she whispered.

“Yes,” Ajay replied. “Of permission.”

They left the hall together.

By midmorning, the first scream cut through routine.

It did not come from the house.

It came from the gardens.

Ajay heard it from a distance, sharp and unrestrained. It broke the estate’s practiced quiet, slicing through order with brutal clarity.

Workers dropped baskets and ran.

Supervisors shouted instructions that dissolved into confusion.

Ajay moved steadily toward the sound.

He did not hurry.

Haste implied resistance.

The land opened around him.

At the dip where the soil darkened and retained moisture longer than elsewhere, a crowd had formed. People stood in uneven clusters, unsure where to position themselves. Fear disrupted hierarchy.

Ajay approached the edge.

A body lay on the ground.

Not hidden.

Not obscured.

Visible.

A man in his forties, face turned upward, eyes open but unseeing. His mouth was slightly parted, as if speech had been interrupted. One hand rested against his chest, fingers curled inward.

Blood was present.

Not excessive.

Contained.

It stained his shirt near the heart, dark and unmistakable.

The sight carried weight.

This death would not be explained away as exhaustion or coincidence.

It announced itself.

Ajay knelt beside the body briefly, careful not to touch.

He did not need to.

The alignment was complete.

The man had been one of the supervisors.

Trusted.

Efficient.

Invisible in importance.

He had spoken once, weeks earlier, in defense of procedure. Of necessity. Of compliance.

Ajay remembered the conversation clearly.

The supervisor had believed order protected everyone.

Order had protected itself.

Ajay stood and stepped back.

Manasa arrived moments later, her breath shallow, eyes fixed on the body.

"This is the one," she said quietly.

"Yes," Ajay replied.

She closed her eyes briefly.

"I felt the blood before I saw it," she said.

"Yes."

Her hands trembled.

"This will not be hidden," she said.

"No," Ajay replied.

The crowd murmured.

Whispers spread quickly, uncontained. Fear traveled faster than instruction. Someone mentioned the lake. Someone else mentioned the painting. The words circulated without structure.

The estate lost coherence.

Supervisors attempted to reassert control, but their voices lacked conviction. Authority fractured when certainty collapsed.

Jaya Lakshmi arrived shortly thereafter.

Her presence did not quiet the crowd.

It unsettled it further.

She approached the body with rigid composure, her face pale but controlled. She did not kneel. She did not look away.

"What happened" she asked.

No one answered immediately.

Finally, one of the workers spoke.

"He collapsed," the worker said. "He was speaking. Then he fell."

"Cause" she asked sharply.

No one responded.

Doctors were summoned. Police informed. Procedures initiated.

But procedures arrived too late to contain narrative.

This death spoke.

Jaya Lakshmi turned toward Ajay.

Her gaze was sharp, accusatory.

"You knew," she said.

"Yes," Ajay replied.

"You allowed this," she said.

"No," Ajay replied. "I witnessed it."

Her hands clenched.

"You bring disorder wherever you stand," she said.

"No," Ajay replied. "Disorder arrives when structure resists memory."

She turned away sharply.

"This ends now," she said. "You will leave the estate."

"Yes," Ajay replied. "When observation concludes."

Her control cracked visibly.

"People are dead," she said. "Because of this madness."

"No," Ajay replied. "They are dead because of **permission** given long ago."

She stared at him, horror and rage colliding.

"You accuse me of murder" she demanded.

"No," Ajay replied. "I accuse you of **allowance**."

The word landed heavily.

Allowance.

The crowd fell silent, drawn by the intensity.

Jaya Lakshmi stepped back as if struck.

"This is manipulation," she said. "Psychological contagion."

"No," Ajay replied. "It is sequence."

The police arrived shortly after.

Statements were taken. Explanations offered. Doctors spoke of cardiac rupture. Stress. Undiagnosed conditions.

The blood complicated everything.

No immediate answers emerged.

The body was removed.

The land absorbed the absence.

That evening, the estate stood fractured.

Workers left early. Machinery shut down unevenly. Lights flickered briefly in the corridors.

The house no longer masked tension.

Jaya Lakshmi retreated to the central hall.

She stood before the covered painting, staring at the concealed shape.

Her breath came unevenly now.

She reached out.

Her hand hovered inches from the cloth.

She did not pull it away.

She did not remove it.

She froze.

Behind her, Ajay stood quietly.

"You can still look," he said.

She did not turn.

"I will not," she said. "I refuse."

"Yes," Ajay replied. "That is clear."

Her shoulders trembled.

"This is not justice," she said.

"No," Ajay replied. "This is **exposure**."

She laughed softly, a sound edged with hysteria.

"You believe the land thinks," she said.

"No," Ajay replied. "I believe memory accumulates."

She turned suddenly, eyes wild.

"How many more" she demanded.

Ajay met her gaze steadily.

"As many as denial sustains," he said.

The silence that followed was heavy, irreversible.

That night, the estate did not sleep.

Lights burned in unexpected rooms. Doors opened and closed without purpose. The lake rippled under still air.

Manasa remained awake, listening.

She felt the sequence advance.

The first death had arrived openly.

It could not be hidden.

It could not be reframed.

It could not be denied.

And now the estate understood something essential.

Silence no longer protected.

Control no longer concealed.

The path ahead had narrowed.

And Jaya Lakshmi stood at its center, surrounded by the consequences she had spent a lifetime allowing.

## *CHAPTER NINETEEN*

## *THE MIND THAT TURNS INWARD*

Jaya Lakshmi did not sleep after the death.

Sleep required surrender, and surrender implied vulnerability. Vulnerability invited collapse. She remained awake through the night, seated in the central hall with the lights dimmed low, staring at the covered painting without touching it.

The house watched.

She could feel that now.

It was not imagination. Imagination softened experience. This sensation sharpened it. Walls felt closer than before. The ceiling pressed downward subtly, not enough to notice at once, but enough to demand awareness. Sound no longer traveled cleanly. It returned distorted, delayed.

The estate had changed its relationship with her.

For the first time since childhood, she felt **alone** within power.

Morning arrived reluctantly. Light crept into the hall unevenly, avoiding the covered canvas as if uncertain how to behave. Shadows clung to corners longer than necessary. Dust motes hung suspended, unmoving.

Jaya Lakshmi rose slowly, joints stiff from hours of stillness. Her body felt heavier than usual, as if gravity had increased overnight. She took a step forward, then another, testing the floor as if it might shift beneath her weight.

It did not.

But it no longer reassured her.

She moved through the bungalow with controlled precision, inspecting rooms that required no inspection. She adjusted a lamp that was already aligned. She straightened a chair no one had touched. These actions did not restore order. They merely delayed awareness.

Control, she realized with growing unease, had become **performative.**

Staff avoided her gaze that morning.

Not deliberately.

Instinctively.

They bowed their heads slightly, murmured responses, moved aside too quickly. Respect had shifted into caution. Authority weakened the moment it required acknowledgment.

She noticed everything.

Heightened awareness was the first sign of fracture.

In the estate office, she reviewed reports without absorbing their content. Numbers blurred. Figures that once reassured her now appeared arbitrary. Profit margins meant nothing in the presence of blood.

She slammed the file shut abruptly.

"This ends today," she said aloud.

The sound of her own voice startled her.

She stood and walked to the window overlooking the gardens. Workers moved carefully, their spacing uneven, their rhythm disrupted. No laughter rose. No casual conversation lingered. Fear had altered geometry.

She felt anger surge.

Anger was familiar.

Anger restored direction.

"They are poisoning this place," she muttered.

The thought arrived uninvited.

Not they as in workers.

They as in **observers**.

Ajay.

Manasa.

The painting.

They had introduced uncertainty.

Uncertainty eroded discipline.

Discipline sustained order.

The logic tightened around her like armor.

She summoned Ajay.

He arrived without haste, his presence unchanged despite the escalation around him. That steadiness infuriated her.

"You will leave today," she said without preamble.

"Yes," Ajay replied. "When observation concludes."

"That time has passed," she said sharply. "Your presence is destabilizing."

"No," Ajay replied calmly. "Your resistance is."

Her hands clenched.

"You manipulate perception," she said. "You encourage hysteria."

"No," Ajay replied. "I **witness** response."

She stepped closer.

"You want me to believe the land thinks," she said.

"No," Ajay replied. "I want you to recognize memory."

"Memory lies," she snapped.

"Memory accumulates," Ajay replied.

She turned away abruptly.

"Everything that has happened since your arrival proves my point," she said. "Deaths. Fear. Disorder."

"Sequence does not require cause," Ajay replied. "Only alignment."

She spun back toward him.

"You speak as if this were inevitable," she said.

"Yes," Ajay replied.

That certainty terrified her.

Certainty without her consent felt like theft.

"You are dangerous," she said.

"No," Ajay replied. "I am **present**."

She dismissed him with a sharp gesture.

"Leave my sight," she said.

Ajay did.

As he walked away, the house seemed to tighten around her.

She felt it immediately.

The corridors felt longer. Turns she had navigated for decades now required conscious thought. Doors appeared unfamiliar, as if subtly relocated. Sound followed her footsteps, echoing back too clearly.

The fracture widened.

That afternoon, she ordered additional security measures. Gates were checked. Patrols increased. Surveillance cameras reviewed repeatedly. She watched recordings obsessively, scanning for patterns that did not exist.

Her mind sought **culprit**.

Culprit simplified narrative.

Without culprit, she would have to face structure.

Manasa appeared briefly at the edge of her awareness near the staircase.

Jaya Lakshmi froze.

"You," she said sharply.

Manasa stopped.

"You see too much," Jaya Lakshmi continued. "Your dreams infect others."

"I do not choose them," Manasa replied softly.

"Choice is irrelevant," Jaya Lakshmi snapped. "Impact matters."

Manasa held her gaze.

"You are afraid," she said.

Fear ignited rage.

"I am not afraid," Jaya Lakshmi said. "I am responsible."

"Responsibility requires **recognition**," Manasa replied.

The word struck her violently.

"Leave," Jaya Lakshmi shouted.

Manasa withdrew without protest.

The house responded.

A loud crack echoed from somewhere above, like wood adjusting under pressure. Dust fell lightly from the ceiling near the portraits. Jaya Lakshmi flinched.

Her breath quickened.

She pressed a hand against her chest, feeling her heart race.

This was not physical illness.

This was **paranoia.**

She knew the word.

She had dismissed it in others countless times.

Paranoia was belief without evidence.

Yet evidence now surrounded her.

The painting remained covered, yet she felt it constantly. Its presence pressed against her awareness even when she stood far from the hall. She sensed its orientation, its position, its refusal.

She began avoiding the central hall entirely.

Avoidance felt like relief at first.

Then it felt like surrender.

At night, she locked her door.

She had never done this before.

The click of the lock echoed too loudly in the quiet room. She sat on the bed, fully clothed, listening to the house breathe.

Breathing.

Yes.

That was the sensation.

The house breathed.

Walls expanded and contracted subtly. Floors creaked rhythmically. Pipes carried sound like distant circulation.

Her mind raced.

She imagined footsteps that were not there. She replayed conversations obsessively, searching for accusation. She scrutinized every interaction for betrayal.

Trust disintegrated rapidly once doubt took root.

She rose and paced the room.

Her reflection in the mirror startled her again.

Her eyes looked unfamiliar.

Sharper.

More desperate.

She turned away.

"I will not be undone by ghosts," she whispered.

The whisper did not reassure her.

Morning brought no relief.

The estate reported another malfunction. A shipment delayed. A machine refusing to restart. Small disruptions that once would have been dismissed now felt targeted.

Targeting implied intelligence.

Intelligence implied intention.

Her thoughts circled relentlessly.

Someone was orchestrating this.

Ajay.

No.

He observed.

Observation alone could not cause collapse.

Unless collapse was already imminent.

The realization struck her suddenly.

The thought made her dizzy.

She sat down heavily, gripping the armrest.

Her chest tightened.

Breath shortened.

Panic rose.

Panic was unacceptable.

She forced herself to breathe slowly, counting each inhale, each exhale. Control returned gradually, but something fundamental had shifted.

She could no longer distinguish between internal threat and external cause.

That was the fracture.

By evening, she returned to the central hall despite herself.

The covered painting loomed larger than before.

She stood several feet away, staring at the cloth.

Her hand trembled again.

"You will not defeat me," she said aloud.

The house did not respond.

Silence felt heavier than any answer.

She imagined uncovering the painting. Imagined confronting it. Imagined reclaiming dominance.

Her hand rose.

Then stopped.

Fear surged.

Not fear of the painting.

Fear of **recognition**.

Recognition would collapse narrative.

Narrative sustained identity.

Without identity, she did not know who she would be.

She stepped back.

The refusal locked something inside her permanently.

That night, she dreamed again.

Not symbol.

Not memory.

She dreamed of corridors folding inward, walls narrowing until movement became impossible. She dreamed of voices whispering her name from behind doors she had sealed long ago.

She woke screaming.

Staff rushed to her door.

She dismissed them harshly, ashamed of exposure.

Exposure weakened authority.

From that moment on, Jaya Lakshmi no longer trusted her own mind.

Thoughts felt intrusive. Sensations felt exaggerated. Sounds felt intentional.

Paranoia settled fully.

The mind that had once imposed order now turned inward, consuming itself.

Ajay observed quietly from a distance.

Manasa felt the pressure intensify.

The estate shifted again.

The next phase had begun.

Control had collapsed into **fear**.

And fear, once established, obeyed no command.

# CHAPTER TWENTY

# THE HOUSE THAT TURNS

The first sign was not sound.

It was **misplacement**.

Jaya Lakshmi reached for the lamp beside her bed and found empty air. The table stood where it always had, the lamp exactly where it should be, yet her hand closed around nothing. She froze, breath suspended, fingers curling reflexively as if the object might reappear through insistence.

She turned her head slowly.

The lamp was there.

Perfectly aligned.

Her hand trembled.

This was not absence.

This was **disobedience**.

She withdrew her hand and sat upright, heart racing. The room felt subtly altered, as if proportions had shifted overnight. The walls seemed closer. The ceiling lower. The air thicker.

She had slept, she realized with shock.

Sleep had claimed her without permission.

That violation unsettled her more than exhaustion would have. Sleep implied surrender. Surrender implied vulnerability.

She rose quickly, dressing with rigid efficiency. The familiar routine did not comfort her. Each movement required conscious effort, as if muscle memory had been erased.

She opened the door and stepped into the corridor.

The corridor did not respond.

It stretched longer than expected, the far end dimmer than memory allowed. Doors along the walls appeared identical, their differences flattened into uniformity. She felt disoriented, though she had walked this path for decades.

Her steps echoed too loudly.

Sound returned to her delayed, distorted, as if the walls reconsidered how to release it.

She stopped.

The house did not correct itself.

It watched.

Jaya Lakshmi swallowed hard and forced herself forward.

As she walked, she noticed small deviations. A window positioned slightly higher than before. A portrait angled differently. A rug she did not remember placing.

None of these were dramatic.

All of them were **undeniable**.

By the time she reached the central hall, her breath was shallow.

The hall was dimmer than usual. Light entered reluctantly, as if filtered through hesitation. Shadows pooled beneath the portraits, deepening their expressions. The covered painting dominated the space without being visible.

She stood at the threshold, unwilling to enter fully.

The hall felt charged.

Not hostile.

Intentional.

"You will not intimidate me," she said aloud.

Her voice sounded thin.

She stepped inside.

The floor felt uneven beneath her feet, though she knew it was not. Each step required recalibration. Distance shifted unpredictably. What appeared near remained unreachable. What appeared far loomed suddenly close.

She felt a sharp pulse of panic.

Panic was unacceptable.

She closed her eyes briefly and counted her breath, forcing rhythm where none existed. The panic receded slightly, leaving behind a hollow tension.

She opened her eyes.

The cloth covering the painting had slipped.

Not fallen.

Shifted.

One corner hung lower than before, revealing a fragment of water beneath.

Her heart lurched.

She crossed the distance before she realized she had moved.

The closer she came, the more the hall resisted her presence. Sound dampened. Air thickened. Her ears rang faintly.

She reached for the cloth.

Her hand stopped inches away.

Not by force.

By **recognition**.

She knew then that touching it would finalize something she had spent her life avoiding.

She withdrew her hand abruptly and stepped back.

The hall responded.

A low creak echoed from above, not sharp enough to identify, not loud enough to locate. The sound traveled through the beams like a message being passed.

She backed away until her shoulders brushed the wall.

Her pulse hammered violently.

The house was no longer passive.

It had begun to **assert**.

She fled the hall.

The corridors seemed to rearrange themselves as she moved, turns appearing where none should exist, familiar paths leading elsewhere. She stopped twice to orient herself, only to find orientation unreliable.

The house had withdrawn cooperation.

She reached the estate office at last, slamming the door shut behind her.

The lock clicked loudly.

The sound echoed back at her, multiplied.

She pressed her back against the door, breathing hard.

"You are imagining this," she whispered.

The whisper offered no reassurance.

Her mind raced, searching for explanation.

Fatigue.

Stress.

Psychological suggestion.

Ajay.

Yes.

This was his doing.

Not through action.

Through **contagion**.

He had seeded doubt. He had destabilized perception. Once doubt entered, the mind complied with it.

That explanation restored a fragment of control.

She straightened her posture and moved to the desk, opening files at random. She forced herself to read, to focus on numbers, on schedules, on logistics.

Reality existed on paper.

Paper did not rearrange itself.

Yet as she read, the words swam. Lines blurred. Figures refused to settle.

Her hands shook.

She slammed the file shut.

"No," she said sharply.

The office responded with silence.

She glanced toward the door, half expecting it to open.

It did not.

But she felt watched.

Not by people.

By **space**.

That afternoon, the house escalated.

A door she had locked opened silently behind her. She turned in time to see it swing inward slowly, as if testing her reaction. She rushed forward and slammed it shut again, her heart racing.

Her breath came in short bursts.

This was no longer subtle.

This was **hostility**.

She summoned staff repeatedly, issuing instructions that contradicted themselves. Curtains were to be drawn, then opened. Doors locked, then unlocked. Lights turned on, then dimmed.

Staff complied outwardly, but fear shadowed their movements. They avoided her gaze, responded too quickly, retreated too soon.

Authority eroded when it demanded constant reinforcement.

Manasa watched from a distance, her face pale.

"This is not safe," Manasa said softly when they crossed paths.

"Do not speak to me," Jaya Lakshmi snapped.

"The house is reacting," Manasa continued. "You are provoking it."

"Do not project your delusions onto me," Jaya Lakshmi shouted.

Manasa stepped back, hurt flickering briefly across her face.

"I feel it," she said. "It is not angry. It is **correcting**."

The word infuriated her.

"There is nothing to correct," Jaya Lakshmi said. "This house exists because of me."

Manasa held her gaze.

"No," she said gently. "You exist because of it."

Jaya Lakshmi raised her hand as if to strike her.

She stopped herself.

Violence would confirm loss of control.

Manasa retreated silently.

As night fell, the house intensified its pressure.

Lights flickered in empty rooms. Footsteps echoed where no one walked. The sound of water carried faintly through walls, though no pipes ran there.

Jaya Lakshmi barricaded herself in her room.

She dragged a chair beneath the door handle, her movements frantic. She sat on the bed, fully clothed, eyes darting toward shadows that seemed to shift independently.

Her mind fractured further.

Every sound acquired intention. Every creak became message. Every shadow suggested movement.

She clutched her head, pressing her palms against her temples.

"Stop," she whispered.

The house did not respond.

It did not need to.

Response had already occurred.

She closed her eyes briefly, seeking escape.

The moment she did, images surged.

Corridors narrowing.

Doors sealing.

The lake rising.

The faces of those she had allowed to disappear.

She screamed and opened her eyes again, breath ragged.

Sleep was impossible.

Time lost coherence.

Hours stretched and collapsed unpredictably. She no longer knew whether it was night or dawn. The house controlled rhythm now.

At some point, she realized something terrifying.

The fear was no longer external.

It was **internalized**.

The house did not need to move.

Her mind completed the movement on its behalf.

That realization broke something essential.

She curled inward on the bed, knees drawn to her chest, rocking slightly.

“I will not confess,” she whispered. “I will not look.”

The refusal echoed hollowly.

The house waited.

Waiting had become active.

By morning, she emerged from the room exhausted, eyes bloodshot, posture slumped. Staff stared openly now, unable to disguise concern.

She no longer commanded space.

She occupied it nervously.

Ajay observed from the veranda, his expression unchanged.

"This is not your doing," Manasa said quietly to him.

"No," Ajay replied. "It is **alignment**."

The house had turned.

Not violently.

Not vindictively.

It had simply withdrawn accommodation.

Space no longer softened for her.

Sound no longer yielded.

Memory no longer receded.

The structure she had relied upon now behaved as witness.

And witness, once awakened, did not return to silence.

# CHAPTER TWENTY ONE

# THE ATTEMPTED EXPULSION

Jaya Lakshmi woke with the certainty that something must be removed.

Not adjusted. Not concealed. Not reframed.

Removed.

The clarity arrived without relief. It pressed against her mind with the sharpness of command, stripping away hesitation. This certainty did not feel like decision. It felt like necessity.

Ajay.

His presence had become intolerable.

Not because he spoke too much. Not because he acted. He did neither. His danger lay in stillness. In the way he occupied space without altering it, allowing others to notice what had already been present.

Stillness exposed.

Exposure dismantled control.

She rose from the bed without looking back at the room. The barricade she had constructed during the night lay displaced, the chair no longer beneath the handle. She did not remember moving it.

The house had decided.

That realization hardened her resolve.

She dressed quickly, her movements clipped and mechanical. Her reflection in the mirror startled her again. The face that looked back was gaunt, eyes rimmed with red, expression tightened into something she did not recognize as her own.

Recognition was not permitted.

She turned away.

As she stepped into the corridor, she noticed that the house had softened slightly. Not welcoming. Neutral. As if it sensed intent and waited to observe outcome.

The corridors no longer shifted unpredictably. Doors remained where they should. Sound traveled normally.

The house was allowing this.

That unsettled her more than resistance would have.

She walked directly to the central hall.

The cloth still covered the painting, though it seemed heavier than before, as if saturated with refusal. She did not approach it. Her attention fixed instead on the empty space where Ajay often stood.

That absence irritated her.

She summoned the estate manager and two senior supervisors. Her voice was steady when she spoke, controlled and precise.

"Ajay will leave today," she said. "Arrangements will be made immediately."

The men exchanged brief glances.

"Yes, madam," one replied.

Their compliance reassured her momentarily.

She proceeded to the estate office and drafted formal termination papers herself. Each word was chosen carefully, stripped of ambiguity. She cited breach of trust, disruption of morale, and professional misconduct. The language was authoritative.

Language restored power.

As she signed her name, the pen hesitated briefly against the paper. A thin line of ink spread unevenly before settling.

She stared at it.

Even writing resisted her now.

She pushed the thought aside and rose.

Ajay was on the veranda overlooking the gardens when she found him. He stood with his hands loosely at his sides, his posture relaxed, his gaze directed toward the distant rows of tea plants.

He did not turn when she approached.

"You will leave the estate today," she said.

"Yes," Ajay replied calmly. "When observation concludes."

"This is not a negotiation," she said sharply.

"No," Ajay replied. "It is a sequence."

Her anger flared.

"You hide behind ambiguity," she said. "You have created hysteria among my staff."

"No," Ajay replied. "They are responding to **memory**."

"Memory is irrelevant," she snapped. "Order is what sustains life here."

"Order sustains itself," Ajay replied. "Life sustains consequence."

She stepped closer.

"You believe yourself untouchable," she said.

"No," Ajay replied. "I believe myself unnecessary."

The words unsettled her.

Unnecessary meant expendable.

Expendable meant removable.

"Then you will go," she said. "Immediately."

"Yes," Ajay replied. "After the next alignment."

She raised her voice.

"There will be no next anything," she said. "I am ending this."

Ajay turned to face her then.

"You are attempting to end **witness**," he said. "Witness is not located in me."

Her breath caught.

She gestured sharply toward the supervisors standing at a distance.

"Escort him out," she commanded.

The men hesitated.

That hesitation lasted only a moment, but it was enough.

Jaya Lakshmi felt it like a physical blow.

"Now," she repeated.

They approached Ajay cautiously.

Ajay did not resist.

He did not move.

He simply stood.

As the first man reached for his arm, a loud crack echoed through the gardens.

Not thunder.

Not machinery.

A sound like earth splitting under pressure.

Everyone froze.

The supervisor withdrew his hand instinctively.

The sound traveled outward, rolling across the estate in a low vibration that unsettled balance. Birds scattered from nearby trees. Workers looked up in alarm.

The land had responded.

Jaya Lakshmi felt the shock ripple through her chest.

"This is coincidence," she said loudly.

"No," Ajay replied softly. "This is **refusal**."

She turned on the supervisors.

"Take him away," she shouted.

They tried again.

This time, as their hands neared Ajay, a sharp pain shot through one man's arm. He cried out and stumbled backward, clutching his wrist. There was no visible injury.

Fear spread quickly.

The second supervisor stepped back, pale.

"I cannot," he said. "Something is wrong."

Rage consumed her.

"You are all weak," she shouted. "This estate exists because of discipline."

The house answered.

A gust of wind tore through the veranda, though the air beyond the gardens remained still. Papers scattered. Doors slammed in distant corridors. The sound of water surged briefly from the direction of the lake.

Jaya Lakshmi staggered.

The house was no longer neutral.

It had taken position.

She pointed at Ajay with a trembling hand.

"Leave," she screamed. "Get out of my sight."

Ajay did not move.

"I will leave," he said calmly. "When the house releases me."

Her knees weakened.

"This is madness," she whispered.

"No," Ajay replied. "This is **completion**."

She turned away abruptly and fled toward the bungalow, her steps unsteady. Staff parted instinctively as she passed. No one attempted to stop her.

Authority had dissolved into spectacle.

She reached the central hall and slammed the door shut behind her. Her chest heaved as she struggled to breathe.

The cloth covering the painting had fallen completely.

The canvas stood revealed.

The water within it appeared darker than before.

She screamed.

"Cover it," she shouted, though no one stood near enough to obey.

Her mind raced.

This was not possible.

Objects did not move themselves.

Houses did not resist command.

Land did not choose.

Unless choice had always existed and she had merely ignored it.

That thought shattered something fragile inside her.

She stumbled backward, colliding with a table, sending objects crashing to the floor. The sound echoed sharply, amplified by the hall's vastness.

She pressed her back against the wall, staring at the painting.

"I built this," she whispered. "I maintained it. I protected it."

The figure in the painting waited.

Waiting was worse than accusation.

She slid down the wall, her body folding inward, breath shallow, heart pounding erratically.

Outside, the estate responded violently now.

A machine in the factory seized and ground to a halt with a scream of metal. Workers scattered. Alarms sounded briefly, then cut out. The gardens rustled without wind.

The attempt to expel Ajay had triggered acceleration.

Manasa felt it from her room, a sharp surge of pressure that nearly knocked her to her knees. She steadied herself against the wall, tears streaming without understanding.

"It has begun," she whispered.

Ajay stood alone on the veranda, watching the estate shift.

"This was inevitable," he said quietly.

By evening, Jaya Lakshmi had locked herself in the central hall.

She refused food. She refused conversation. She refused acknowledgment.

Denial hardened into isolation.

Isolation intensified collapse.

The house did not force entry.

It waited.

The failed expulsion had proven something irreversible.

Control could not remove witness.

Authority could not expel consequence.

And resistance, once made visible, only sharpened what followed.

# CHAPTER TWENTY TWO

# THE ALIGNMENT OF WITNESS

The estate did not calm after the failed expulsion.

It clarified.

This distinction mattered, though few would have recognized it. Calm suggested resolution. Clarification suggested direction. The land did not soften its posture. It refined it, stripping away ambiguity until only intention remained.

Ajay felt the shift before he saw any outward sign. The pressure he had carried quietly since his arrival no longer pressed inward. It leveled. Balance replaced tension, not because danger had passed, but because sequence had reached coherence.

Hene did not celebrate this change.

Completion was not triumph.

It was inevitability.

He walked away from the veranda and toward the lower paths leading to the lake. The air felt heavier than before, yet breathable. Each step landed with precision, as if the ground anticipated his weight.

Behind him, the bungalow stood unsettled, its windows dark despite the daylight. The central hall remained sealed from within. Jaya Lakshmi had not emerged. Her isolation had become structural.

Manasa waited near the banyan tree at the edge of the gardens. She had not chosen the spot consciously. Her body had moved there without deliberation, guided by a pull she no longer questioned.

When she saw Ajay approach, something inside her steadied.

"You felt it," she said.

"Yes," Ajay replied.

“It is different now,” she said. “Sharper.”

“Yes.”

She looked toward the lake, its surface unusually still.

“I am afraid,” she admitted quietly.

“Yes,” Ajay replied. “Fear is appropriate.”

She exhaled slowly.

“I used to think fear meant danger,” she said. “Now it feels like instruction.”

Ajay nodded.

“Fear becomes guidance when resistance ends,” he said.

They stood together in silence for a moment, listening to the estate adjust around them. Sound traveled differently now. Not distorted. Directed. Each noise carried meaning through placement rather than volume.

“What happens next” Manasa asked.

“Acceleration,” Ajay replied.

She closed her eyes briefly.

“That word frightens me,” she said.

“It should,” Ajay replied. “Acceleration removes delay.”

She looked at him.

“Delay protected her,” she said.

“Yes,” Ajay replied. “Delay protected many.”

The lake rippled faintly, though no wind touched it.

Manasa felt the pull again.

"I see it now," she said. "Not images. Not dreams. Patterns."

"Yes," Ajay replied.

"They are not random," she continued. "They are shaped by **allowance**."

Ajay did not interrupt.

"The land waited because it was told to wait," she said. "By her. By the structure she maintained."

"Yes."

"And when waiting no longer served balance," Manasa added, "it moved."

"Yes."

She shuddered.

"This is larger than her," she said.

"Yes," Ajay replied. "But it requires her."

They turned toward the bungalow together.

Inside the central hall, Jaya Lakshmi sat against the wall opposite the painting. She had not slept. Her eyes burned with exhaustion, her body rigid with tension. The hall felt vast around her, its emptiness amplifying her isolation.

The painting stood fully revealed now.

She no longer looked at it directly.

Looking implied engagement.

Engagement implied surrender.

She stared instead at the floor, tracing familiar patterns in the stone that no longer comforted her. The sound of the house surrounded her, not loud but omnipresent. Wood adjusted. Walls breathed. The ceiling creaked softly.

She pressed her palms against her temples.

"This is not real," she whispered.

The whisper dissolved into silence.

Silence did not contradict her.

It waited.

Footsteps approached.

She stiffened.

Ajay entered the hall calmly, Manasa just behind him. They did not rush. They did not hesitate. Their presence altered the air immediately.

Jaya Lakshmi looked up, fury flashing briefly through exhaustion.

"You have no right," she said hoarsely.

"Yes," Ajay replied.

The word confused her.

"Yes" she demanded.

"Yes you are right," Ajay replied. "Rights no longer apply here."

She laughed sharply.

"Then what does" she asked.

"**Recognition**," Ajay replied.

She pushed herself to her feet, swaying slightly.

"You think this ends with confession," she said. "With apology."

"No," Ajay replied. "It ends with alignment."

She stared at him.

"I will not confess," she said.

"No one has asked you to," Ajay replied.

Manasa stepped forward slightly.

"You do not need to speak," she said softly. "You need to **see**."

Jaya Lakshmi recoiled.

"I see enough," she snapped.

"No," Manasa replied. "You see structure. Not consequence."

Her breath quickened.

"This is cruelty," she said. "You want to break me."

"No," Ajay replied. "Breaking occurs when resistance exceeds capacity."

She looked at the painting then despite herself.

The water within it appeared deeper now, darker, as if it had absorbed years of withheld memory. The figure beside it no longer waited passively. Its posture suggested readiness, not action but completion.

She felt something inside her give way.

Not fully.

Enough.

"You believe the land judges me," she said weakly.

"No," Ajay replied. "The land mirrors **sequence**."

She shook her head.

"I protected this place," she whispered. "I preserved it."

"Yes," Ajay replied. "At the cost of inclusion."

Her chest tightened.

"That man," she said suddenly. "The one from the gardens. He was undisciplined."

"Yes," Ajay replied.

"He disrupted order," she continued. "He threatened stability."

"Yes," Ajay replied.

She looked at him sharply.

"Then you admit it," she said. "I was right."

"No," Ajay replied. "I acknowledge your logic."

She sagged slightly.

"Logic is not innocence," Manasa said gently. "It is justification."

Jaya Lakshmi covered her face with her hands.

"I did not push him," she whispered.

"No," Ajay replied. "You **allowed**."

The word struck with quiet force.

Allowance.

She lowered her hands slowly.

"And my brother" she asked.

"You withheld belonging," Ajay replied.

"And the workers" she continued.

"You prioritized structure over life," Ajay replied.

Her breath shook.

"This never ends," she said.

"No," Ajay replied. "It completes."

She looked at Manasa.

"What happens to me" she asked.

Manasa hesitated.

"You remain," she said. "With what you see."

Jaya Lakshmi laughed softly, broken.

"That is punishment," she said.

"No," Ajay replied. "That is **continuity**."

The hall reacted.

A deep sound rolled through the structure, not violent but decisive. The portraits along the walls seemed to darken uniformly. The light shifted, settling fully on the painting.

Jaya Lakshmi felt it then.

The house was no longer addressing her authority.

It was addressing her presence.

She stood unsteadily and took a step toward the painting.

Ajay did not stop her.

Manasa held her breath.

Each step felt heavier than the last. Her legs trembled. Her vision blurred.

She stood before the canvas at last.

The water within it moved.

Not visibly.

Internally.

She saw then what she had refused for decades.

Not faces.

Not accusations.

Chains of decision.

Moments of silence.

Choices framed as necessity.

Lives narrowed until disappearance felt natural.

Tears streamed down her face.

"I thought I was strong," she whispered.

"You were," Ajay replied. "Strength without reflection becomes **exclusion**."

She sank to her knees.

The house exhaled slowly.

Not in relief.

In confirmation.

Outside, the estate adjusted again. Machinery fell silent briefly, then restarted smoothly. The wind passed through the gardens evenly. The lake rippled once, then settled.

Acceleration had reached its threshold.

Not toward chaos.

Toward balance.

Manasa felt the pressure ease slightly.

"It is aligning," she said.

"Yes," Ajay replied.

Jaya Lakshmi remained kneeling, her shoulders shaking.

"What now" she asked faintly.

Ajay looked around the hall, at the portraits, at the painting, at the woman who had shaped the estate through decades of controlled absence.

"Now you live," he said. "With **recognition**."

She nodded weakly.

Living had never frightened her before.

It did now.

The estate did not close in.

It opened.

Not gently.

Not cruelly.

It opened as systems do when correction replaces denial.

Ajay turned toward the exit.

Manasa followed.

Behind them, the house settled into a new rhythm.

Not silent.

Honest.

The witness had aligned with the future.

And alignment, once achieved, did not retreat.

# CHAPTER TWENTY THREE

# WHAT REMAINS AFTER CONTROL

Morning arrived without ceremony.

There was no dramatic shift in light, no thunderous declaration from the sky. The estate simply woke into itself, as it always had. Yet something essential had altered during the night. The air felt lighter, not because danger had passed, but because resistance had loosened its grip.

Ajay sensed it as he stepped onto the veranda.

The pressure that had accompanied him for weeks had thinned. Not vanished. Transformed. Where it once pressed inward, it now flowed outward, dispersing through the land like breath finally released after long restraint.

The estate was no longer asking questions.

It had accepted answers.

Below him, the gardens moved with renewed coherence. Workers walked with steadier rhythm. Conversations resumed in low tones, cautious but no longer fractured. The land responded to touch again, no longer tense beneath hands that feared consequence.

Balance had begun to return.

Not balance as comfort.

Balance as **truth**.

Manasa joined him quietly. Her posture had changed since the night before. She stood more fully within herself now, no longer braced against unseen pressure.

"It is quieter," she said.

"Yes," Ajay replied.

"Not empty," she added.

"No," Ajay said. "Aligned."

She looked toward the central hall windows.

"She is still there," Manasa said.

"Yes."

"She will not leave easily," Manasa continued. "Control does not dissolve overnight."

"No," Ajay replied. "It withdraws gradually."

They stood in silence for a moment longer.

"What happens to the estate now" Manasa asked.

Ajay considered the question carefully.

"It stops belonging to one person," he said. "It begins belonging to consequence."

Manasa frowned slightly.

"That sounds dangerous," she said.

"It is honest," Ajay replied.

Inside the central hall, Jaya Lakshmi remained seated on the floor before the painting.

She had not moved since the previous night.

Her body ached. Her joints protested stillness. Her eyes burned from lack of sleep. Yet she did not rise.

Movement felt inappropriate.

The painting stood before her, no longer accusatory, no longer demanding. It simply existed. The water within it appeared calmer than before, darker but settled.

She felt hollow.

Not emptied.

Rearranged.

For the first time in her life, the estate did not respond to her presence. It neither recoiled nor submitted. It allowed her to exist within it without confirmation.

That neutrality frightened her.

Control had always offered feedback.

Neutrality offered none.

She placed her palm flat against the cool stone floor.

"I do not know how to live like this," she whispered.

The hall did not respond.

It did not need to.

By midmorning, the first delegation arrived.

Managers. Supervisors. Account officers. People who had once deferred automatically now approached with visible hesitation. Not defiance. Caution.

They stood at a respectful distance.

"Madam," one of them said gently, "we need guidance."

The word struck her sharply.

Guidance implied movement.

Movement implied leadership.

Leadership implied responsibility she no longer trusted herself to wield.

She looked up slowly.

"What kind of guidance" she asked.

The man hesitated.

"There are concerns," he said. "About decision structures. About oversight. About… continuity."

Continuity.

That word once belonged to her.

Now it sounded foreign.

She closed her eyes briefly.

"Continue operations," she said finally. "As they are."

The man nodded uncertainly.

"And governance" he asked.

She opened her eyes.

"Governance must expand," she said quietly. "I will not be the sole point of control."

The words felt heavy.

But they felt **true**.

The group exchanged glances.

"Yes, madam," they said.

As they left, she felt something loosen inside her chest. Not relief. Permission.

Permission to step back.

Outside, Ajay observed the subtle shift ripple outward.

Decisions no longer waited exclusively for her approval. Small choices were made collaboratively. Minor adjustments occurred without escalation. Authority redistributed itself organically.

This redistribution did not weaken the estate.

It strengthened it.

Manasa noticed it too.

"They are not afraid in the same way," she said.

"No," Ajay replied. "Fear has lost its anchor."

She thought of the dreams that had plagued her for months.

"They have stopped," she said softly.

"Yes," Ajay replied. "Dreams announce imbalance. Balance requires no announcement."

She exhaled slowly.

"What about her" she asked.

Ajay looked toward the hall.

"She will remain," he said. "But she will no longer decide alone."

That afternoon, Jaya Lakshmi walked the estate for the first time without entourage.

No guards. No supervisors. No staff trailing behind her. She walked slowly, her pace uncertain at first, then steadier.

The gardens received her differently.

Plants did not recoil beneath her gaze. Workers did not freeze. Some nodded politely. Others continued their tasks without interruption.

Indifference stung.

Yet it also freed her.

She stopped near the lake.

The water lay calm, reflecting the sky without distortion. For the first time in years, she approached its edge without calculation.

She knelt slowly, knees protesting, and touched the surface lightly.

The water rippled outward gently, then settled.

No accusation.

No memory rising.

Only presence.

Tears slid silently down her cheeks.

"I am still here," she whispered.

Yes.

She was.

But the estate was no longer shaped around her survival.

It was shaped around **continuation**.

That evening, Ajay prepared to leave.

Not ceremonially.

Not announced.

Departure did not require drama.

Manasa found him near the gate.

"You are going," she said.

"Yes," Ajay replied.

"Because it is over" she asked.

"No," Ajay replied. "Because it continues without me."

She smiled faintly.

"I will miss your silence," she said.

"Yes," Ajay replied.

She hesitated.

"What will I do now" she asked.

"You will listen," Ajay replied. "Without fear."

She nodded.

"And her" she asked quietly.

Ajay looked back once more toward the bungalow.

"She will live with **recognition**," he said. "That is not punishment. That is inheritance."

Manasa watched him walk away, his figure dissolving into distance without resistance.

The estate did not react.

It did not need to.

Ajay had never been the source.

He had been the alignment.

Days passed.

Then weeks.

The estate stabilized into a new rhythm.

Committees replaced solitary command. Transparency replaced silence. Memory was acknowledged, not suppressed. Stories surfaced quietly. Some painful. Some long overdue.

No further deaths occurred.

The lake remained still.

The painting remained in the hall, uncovered.

Visitors sometimes paused before it, sensing its gravity without understanding why. No explanations were offered.

Explanation diluted impact.

Jaya Lakshmi no longer stood before it daily.

Sometimes she avoided it.

Sometimes she faced it briefly, then turned away.

She was learning.

Learning was unfamiliar territory.

One evening, she sat alone in the hall and spoke aloud.

"I thought control meant strength," she said.

The words echoed softly.

"Now I see it meant fear."

The hall accepted the statement.

She did not ask forgiveness.

She did not seek absolution.

She simply **recognized**.

Outside, the estate breathed evenly.

The future no longer required her permission.

And in that realization, something gentler than control took root.

Responsibility.

Not imposed.

Shared.

The estate moved forward.

Not cleansed.

Not redeemed.

But honest.

And honesty, once established, proved far more enduring than any structure built on silence.

# CHAPTER TWENTY FOUR

# THOSE WHO WERE NOT COUNTED

The change did not arrive through announcement.

It arrived through **permission**.

Not permission granted by authority, but permission taken by those who had waited long enough to recognize its absence. The estate did not resist this shift. It absorbed it the way land absorbs rain after drought, without celebration, without refusal.

Morning found the gardens alive in a way that felt unfamiliar. Workers gathered not in tight lines but in loose circles, discussing tasks before beginning them. There was no confusion. There was deliberation. Decisions formed organically, shaped by experience rather than instruction.

Manasa watched from a distance.

She had learned not to interfere.

Interference implied direction. Direction implied control. Control belonged to a past that no longer governed the present. She observed quietly as a younger supervisor listened to an older picker describe soil fatigue in a neglected section of the eastern slope. The conversation ended not with command, but with agreement.

Agreement carried **weight**.

The land responded quickly.

Within days, yield stabilized in sections long considered unpredictable. Paths were adjusted. Work hours shifted slightly to match the rhythm of heat rather than clock. Small changes accumulated into visible improvement.

No one took credit.

Credit required ownership.

Ownership had become suspect.

Inside the bungalow, Jaya Lakshmi felt the absence of command acutely. She moved through rooms that no longer waited for her instruction. Staff greeted her politely but did not pause expectantly. Conversations continued when she passed.

This neutrality unsettled her at first.

Then it steadied her.

She had lived surrounded by reaction for so long that its absence felt like silence. Silence required adjustment. Adjustment required humility.

Humility was unfamiliar.

She found herself sitting more often, listening rather than speaking. Listening not for leverage, but for understanding. The difference startled her.

One afternoon, she overheard two workers discussing the old garden manager who had died years ago. They spoke quietly, not with anger, but with acknowledgment. His methods had been flawed, they said, but his commitment had been real. The conversation did not halt when she approached.

They did not ask permission to remember.

She continued walking, her chest tightening slightly.

This was what had been withheld.

Memory without hierarchy.

That evening, she entered the central hall alone.

The painting waited.

She stood before it for a long time without sitting. Her posture remained rigid at first, shoulders drawn inward. Gradually, tension eased. Her breath slowed.

She did not search the image for accusation.

She allowed it to exist.

The water within the canvas appeared calm now, its darkness settled into depth rather than threat. The figure beside it no longer suggested waiting. It suggested arrival.

She understood then.

The painting had never been about judgment.

It had been about **counting**.

Counting those who had been excluded. Counting those who had been allowed to disappear through silence rather than force. Counting what had been deferred rather than denied.

She whispered quietly.

“I did not count you.”

The hall accepted the words without response.

Outside, the estate continued its quiet transformation.

Committees formed naturally, not by decree. Roles adjusted based on skill rather than lineage. Stories surfaced during breaks and meals, fragments of the past spoken without fear of repercussion.

Manasa felt her dreams change.

They no longer announced disaster. They did not carry urgency. Instead, they offered glimpses of connection. Faces she had seen only in passing now appeared with clarity. Not warnings. Invitations.

She dreamed of hands planting together. Of voices blending without dominance. Of water reflecting sky rather than weight.

When she woke, she felt rested.

Ajay did not return.

He was not expected to.

Presence had done its work.

Weeks passed.

Then months.

The estate began exporting under a collective banner rather than a single name. Contracts reflected shared responsibility. Profits were reinvested locally. Training programs emerged without instruction, initiated by those who had once followed without question.

The land thrived.

Not excessively.

Sustainably.

Jaya Lakshmi attended meetings occasionally. She spoke rarely. When she did, her words were measured and brief. She no longer defended decisions reflexively. She asked questions instead.

Questions altered power.

One afternoon, she was asked to approve a proposal to rename a section of the gardens after the old manager who had drowned years ago.

Her breath caught.

The request was not accusatory.

It was **inclusive**.

She considered it carefully.

"Yes," she said finally. "But not as apology."

The group looked at her.

"As acknowledgment," she continued. "He belonged."

They nodded.

Belonging was no longer conditional.

The renaming occurred quietly.

No ceremony.

No speeches.

Just a change on a map and a shift in language.

Language mattered.

The lake remained still.

Children began playing near it again, supervised but unafraid. Its surface reflected laughter now, not memory. The water had completed its work.

Manasa walked there often.

She felt gratitude without relief.

Gratitude implied gift.

This felt earned.

One evening, she sat near the lake as dusk settled and considered the painting. She realized something then that startled her.

The painting no longer needed interpretation.

Its work had moved beyond representation into **inheritance**.

Those who were once invisible now carried the estate forward. Not as owners. As participants.

Jaya Lakshmi visited the lake at dawn one morning alone.

She stood at the edge, watching light break across the surface. She did not kneel. She did not touch the water.

She spoke quietly.

"I am learning to step aside."

The words felt fragile.

But they held.

Stepping aside did not mean disappearance.

It meant making space.

The estate accepted that offering.

By the end of the season, the painting was moved.

Not removed.

Relocated.

It was placed in a smaller hall near the gardens where workers passed daily. No plaque explained it. No title named it. People paused before it briefly, then continued.

That was enough.

The painting had fulfilled its role.

It no longer needed isolation.

Jaya Lakshmi attended the relocation without comment. She watched as the canvas settled into its new space, surrounded by life rather than hierarchy.

Her chest ached.

Not with regret.

With **recognition**.

The estate did not belong to her anymore.

It belonged to those who carried it.

That understanding did not diminish her.

It clarified her.

She returned to the bungalow and closed the door gently behind her. The house felt quieter now, not empty, but resolved.

Outside, voices rose and fell naturally.

Work continued.

Memory remained.

And the future unfolded without asking permission.

The painting stood where it could be seen by those who mattered most.

Those who had not been counted.

Now counted.

Not by power.

By presence.

## CHAPTER TWENTY FIVE

## WHAT WATCHES AND WALKS AWAY

Ajay did not think of departure as leaving.

Leaving suggested attachment. It implied loss, rupture, or unfinished exchange. What he experienced instead was release. A loosening of alignment that did not break connection, but rendered it unnecessary.

He walked away from the estate before sunrise, not because secrecy mattered, but because stillness did. Dawn softened outlines. It reduced certainty without erasing direction. The path beyond the gates curved gently downward, leading into forest that did not belong to anyone.

He welcomed that.

The air felt lighter with each step. The pressure that had accompanied him for months dissolved gradually, dispersing into the land behind him. Not because the work was forgotten, but because it no longer required containment.

Completion did not follow him.

It remained.

He paused briefly at a bend in the path and looked back once.

The estate rested quietly against the slope, gardens unfolding evenly, roofs catching first light. No sound reached him. No call followed. The land did not acknowledge his gaze.

That neutrality confirmed what he already knew.

Witness was no longer required there.

Ajay turned and continued walking.

As the forest closed around him, memory surfaced without weight. Faces appeared briefly, then receded. Moments aligned, then released. He did not cling to them. He had learned long ago that memory, once acknowledged, preferred freedom.

He reached the road by midmorning and accepted a ride from a passing truck without conversation. The driver spoke briefly about weather and distance. Ajay listened without comment. Listening did not always require response.

By evening, he arrived in a town that did not know him.

That anonymity felt correct.

He rented a small room above a closed shop. The walls were plain. The window overlooked a narrow street. The bed creaked softly when he sat. Nothing waited of him there.

That night, he slept deeply.

No dreams arrived.

Dreams belonged to imbalance.

In the days that followed, he moved through the town without purpose. He ate when hungry. Walked when restless. Sat when tired. Time reasserted itself gradually, no longer bent around urgency.

He noticed small things.

A woman watering plants at dawn with careful attention. A child tracing patterns in dust without instruction. A man repairing a broken chair patiently rather than replacing it.

These observations did not accumulate.

They passed through him.

One afternoon, Ajay felt a familiar pressure stir briefly. Not insistence. Recognition. He turned down a narrow lane and found himself standing before an old building scheduled for demolition. Its windows were boarded unevenly. Its walls bore marks of long use.

Inside, he sensed something unresolved.

He did not enter.

He did not need to.

Witness did not require proximity.

He walked away.

Elsewhere, at the estate, Manasa felt the final echo of his departure without knowing its cause. She stood near the gardens as wind moved gently through the leaves. A sensation passed through her chest, subtle and unremarkable.

Completion.

She smiled faintly and returned to her work.

Her days had grown quieter. She no longer woke with urgency. Her dreams, when they came, carried no instruction. They wandered through ordinary spaces, observing life without commentary.

She had learned to trust silence.

One evening, she sat near the relocated painting as workers passed nearby. None paused deliberately. Some glanced briefly. Others ignored it entirely. The painting no longer demanded attention.

That was its fulfillment.

Manasa realized then that she could leave the estate one day if she chose. Not in escape. In expansion. The thought did not frighten her.

Choice felt different now.

At the bungalow, Jaya Lakshmi continued to adjust.

Adjustment was not linear.

Some days she reverted to old habits, issuing directives too quickly, correcting when no correction was needed. When this happened, she noticed it sooner. She paused. She listened.

Listening remained difficult.

But it no longer felt threatening.

She spent long hours in the smaller hall where the painting now hung, not standing before it, but sitting nearby. She watched people pass. She listened to voices rise and fall naturally.

She noticed that the painting no longer drew her attention.

That unsettled her at first.

Then it comforted her.

The need to be seen had dissolved.

One afternoon, a young supervisor approached her hesitantly.

"Madam," he said, "we are considering expanding the cooperative model further."

She nodded.

"Proceed," she said.

No justification followed.

No oversight demanded.

She returned to her seat.

The estate did not falter.

That realization carried quiet power.

Months passed.

Seasons shifted.

The tea harvest adapted to weather patterns rather than schedule. Exports stabilized. Local schools received funding without ceremony. Stories of the past continued to surface, not as accusation, but as acknowledgment.

The lake remained calm.

Sometimes Jaya Lakshmi walked there alone.

She no longer knelt.

She stood.

Standing felt appropriate.

"I did not know how to stop," she said quietly one morning.

The water reflected sky without response.

Response was no longer required.

Elsewhere, Ajay received a letter forwarded from the estate.

He recognized the handwriting immediately.

Manasa's.

He opened it without urgency.

She wrote simply.

Things are steady. People are learning. I am learning too. I think this is what you meant by continuation.

He folded the letter carefully and placed it beside the window.

No reply was necessary.

Witness did not require correspondence.

One evening, as dusk settled over the town, Ajay sat on the steps outside the shop and watched shadows lengthen across the street. A stray dog lay nearby, asleep without concern.

Ajay felt gratitude without attachment.

This was rare.

Gratitude often clung.

This did not.

He understood then that his work had never been about intervention. It had been about **presence**. Presence offered alignment. Alignment invited consequence. Consequence required endurance.

Endurance no longer required him.

He stood and walked back inside.

The light faded.

The town settled.

Life continued.

At the estate, the painting caught the last light of evening briefly, its surface glowing softly before shadow reclaimed it. The figure beside the water no longer suggested waiting or arrival.

It simply existed.

That was enough.

The estate moved forward without asking permission.

Memory remained without pressure.

Control had dissolved into responsibility.

Responsibility into participation.

Participation into continuity.

And continuity, once achieved, required no witness.

Only those willing to live within it.

9 789357 735414

Printed at Repro India Ltd.